The Karate Princess

Jeremy Strong once worked in a bakery, putting the jam into three thousand doughnuts every night. Now he puts the jam in stories instead, which he finds much more exciting. At the age of three, he fell out of a first-floor bedroom window and landed on his head. His mother says that this damaged him for the rest of his life and refuses to take any responsibility. He loves writing stories because he says it is 'the only time you alone have complete control and can make anything happen'. His ambition is to make you laugh (or at least snuffle). Jeremy Strong lives near Bath with his wife, Gillie, four cats and a flying cow.

Are you feeling silly enough to read more?

LAUGH YOUR SOCKS OFF WITH

Jeremy STRONG

The Karate Princess

Illustrated by

Simone Abel

PUFFIN

PUFFIN BOOKS

Published by the Penguin Group
Penguin Books Ltd, 80 Strand, London WC2R ORL, England
Penguin Group (USA) Inc., 375 Hudson Street, New York, New York 10014, USA
Penguin Group (Canada), 90 Eglinton Avenue East, Suite 700, Toronto, Ontario, Canada M4P 2Y3
(a division of Pearson Penguin Canada Inc.)
Penguin Ireland, 25 St Stephen's Green, Dublin 2, Ireland (a division of Penguin Books Ltd)
Penguin Group (Australia), 250 Camberwell Road, Camberwell, Victoria 3124, Australia
(a division of Pearson Australia Group Pty Ltd)
Penguin Books India Pvt Ltd, 11 Community Centre,
Panchsheel Park, New Delhi – 110 017, India
Penguin Group (NZ), 67 Apollo Drive, Rosedale, Auckland 0632, New Zealand
(a division of Pearson New Zealand Ltd)
Penguin Books (South Africa) (Pty) Ltd, 24 Sturdee Avenue,
Rosebank, Johannesburg 2196, South Africa

Penguin Books Ltd, Registered Offices: 80 Strand, London WC2R ORL, England

puffinbooks.com

First published by A&C Black (Publishers) Ltd 1986
First published in Puffin Books 1989
Published in this flip-book edition 2011
003

Text copyright © Jeremy Strong, 1986
Illustrations copyright © Simone Abel, 1986
All rights reserved

The moral right of the author and illustrator has been asserted

Set in Linotron 202 Bembo
Made and printed in Great Britain by Clays Ltd, St Ives plc

British Library Cataloguing in Publication Data
A CIP catalogue record for this book is available from the British Library

ISBN: 978-0-141-33616-9

www.greenpenguin.co.uk

MIX
Paper from
responsible sources
FSC
www.fsc.org
FSC™ C018179

Penguin Books is committed to a sustainable
future for our business, our readers and our planet.
This book is made from Forest Stewardship
Council™ certified paper.

ALWAYS LEARNING   **PEARSON**

The sixteenth princess

When Belinda was born her father, King Stormbelly, took one look at her and said, 'Ugh!' Belinda's mother smiled mildly and observed that princesses never looked their best at two o'clock in the morning, especially when they were only one hour old. As for Belinda, she let out such an almighty wail that the king stuffed his fingers in his ears and fled back to bed.

As time went by Belinda lost her creased-up wrinkles and began to look altogether more attractive, though never beautiful. King Stormbelly decided that something had gone wrong with the child. He had sixteen children. They were all girls, they were all princesses and they were all astonishingly beautiful and talented . . . all except for Belinda, who was quite ordinary. But she did have eyes of a most serene blue. The king never seemed to notice Belinda's eyes.

'I don't know what we're going to do about her,' grumbled King Stormbelly, as

Belinda grew up and showed no signs of becoming a ravishing beauty. 'All the other princesses will find husbands easily, but nobody will be foolish enough to marry her. She's not even particularly clever.'

The queen didn't say anything because she knew that if she started to argue, Stormbelly would just fly into one of his silly tempers, start kicking the guards and hurt his feet on their heavy armour. Then he'd take to his bed and stay there for a week pretending all his toes were broken and it was all the queen's fault.

So the queen didn't say anything, but she thought a great deal. She was very fond of *all* her daughters and especially pleased that fifteen of them were astonishingly beautiful. But she was even more pleased that Belinda was different. What's more, she knew that Belinda was a lot cleverer than her father and it was only because Belinda always beat her father playing 'Snap!' that the king was so grumpy about her.

All the same, the king was quite right when he said that the fifteen beautiful princesses would easily find husbands, whereas Belinda would have to do a bit of work if she ever wanted to marry. The queen thought about all these things and then decided what ought to be done.

First of all she went to Belinda very quietly and whispered in her ear, 'Belinda dear, the next time you play "Snap!" with your father please make sure that you lose.'

'Oh, Mum!' Belinda didn't like losing at anything. 'Do I have to?'

The queen nodded and Belinda sighed, but the next time she played a game with her father she lost.

'Snap!' cried Stormbelly triumphantly. 'Ha, ha! You've got to have sharp eyes to beat me, Belinda.'

'Yes, Dad. I can see that,' the youngest princess murmured shamefacedly.

Off went the king, singing and dancing down the palace corridors, swinging round on the arms of the astonished guards and

making them dance with him, until at last he reached the queen.

'You seem very cheerful, dear,' she mused.

'Ha, ha! Do you know I've just won a game of "Snap!" Old sharp eyes, that's me!' He held his big belly and laughed.

The queen smiled too. 'Oh, I am pleased.'

'Ah,' said the king, sitting down with a soft thud. 'She's not such a bad girl, Belinda.'

'I've been thinking that too, dear. Do you know, I thought it might be a good idea to get her a tutor.' The queen folded her neat little hands in her lap and smiled at the king.

'A tutor?' queried the king. 'Do you mean a teacher?'

'Yes, if you like. A teacher.'

'Whatever for?' demanded Stormbelly gruffly.

'Well, to teach her, of course.'

'Yes, yes. I know that. But what's the point?'

'I know that you have been very worried about Belinda and what will happen to her when she's older. I thought that if she was taught, then she would stand a better chance later on of finding a husband.'

King Stormbelly frowned and twisted his whiskers and scratched his head and snorted a bit. They were all signs that he hadn't got the foggiest idea what he was supposed to be thinking about.

'I don't see how having a teacher will help,' he ventured.

'All the other princesses are beautiful and accomplished and will easily find husbands,' explained the queen. 'But Belinda will have to find hers with her brain, if she wants one.'

'Of course she wants one! Whoever heard of a princess who didn't want a husband?' snapped Stormbelly.

'Anyway,' continued the queen, choosing to ignore the king's last remark, 'we ought to do something about Belinda's brain to help her. Don't you think?'

Stormbelly didn't think very much but it seemed to make sense. And he didn't want Belinda to find things difficult later on. She was a good girl – he'd just beaten her at 'Snap!' and that proved it. He gave a small grunt.

'All right. Good idea. Make the arrangements and get her a teacher.'

So it was that Hiro Ono came to the palace. Hundreds of people from everywhere applied for the post of teacher to the Princess Belinda (it was highly paid), and the queen had private conversations with them all. For days there was a queue over a mile long, stretching out of the palace gates and right

down into the town. The interviews lasted for over a week and at the end of it the queen announced that Hiro Ono, master tutor from Japan, would be Belinda's new teacher.

Belinda wasn't very happy about it. She didn't like the look of Hiro Ono, with his strange silk robe that had red and green dragons swirling around on it, and his thin eyes and bent back. He had a wispy beard too, like an old spider's web caught on his chin. But Hiro Ono smiled at her, and bowed, and they went away together to begin their classes.

The years passed and Stormbelly hardly saw Belinda. In fact, he almost forgot about

her altogether. The queen didn't. She visited
Belinda and Hiro Ono every day to see how
they were getting on, and day by day Belinda
became more and more fond of Hiro Ono
because he taught her such fascinating things.

The other fifteen daughters got married,
one by one, each to a rich and handsome
prince, and went off to start new lives in their
husbands' castles. Stormbelly's castle began
to seem quite empty and all at once he realized that somewhere in the vast palace he had
a sixteenth daughter who wasn't at all beautiful but it was time she got married. He sent
for Belinda.

She and her mother arrived with Hiro Ono

trailing softly behind them, a little more bent with age and his beard a little longer. Belinda had changed too. She was slim and much taller, and her blue eyes were as clear as the blue of a winter sky. Her black hair was cut short, and she regarded her father with a little smile.

'Well,' declared the king. 'How you've grown!' Belinda nodded. 'I hear you've been taught a great deal over the last seven years.'

'Yes, Father,' said Belinda gently.

'Hmmm. Very useful thing, knowledge. So – you've learnt lots and lots. Well now, tell me, um, what are three sixes?'

Belinda shrugged. 'I don't know.'

'You don't know!' King Stormbelly was cross. He had hoped she would be able to tell him because he didn't know the answer himself. Belinda turned to Hiro Ono.

'Do you know what three sixes are?' she asked.

'I know what they aren't,' he said slowly. 'They aren't a husband. They are not a palace. Nor are they happiness. They are not the clouds enclosing the mighty head of a mountain . . .'

'What is he going on about?' burst out the king. 'Is he mad?'

The queen gently touched her husband on the arm. 'I think it is Hiro Ono's way of telling you that it doesn't matter what three sixes are. They are not important.'

'Not important! But I've always wanted to know what three sixes are! All right, then, let's see how much this nitwit has taught Belinda. Daughter, tell me, what's the capital city of Rome?'

The queen nudged him. 'Rome *is* a capital city,' she whispered.

'Oh, all right. What's the capital city of Spain?'

Belinda couldn't answer that either and Stormbelly began to hop from one foot to the other. The queen could see that he was getting ready to kick a few guards and probably Hiro Ono himself.

'Why don't you ask Belinda to show you what she *can* do?' she suggested sweetly.

'Fine, fine. Go ahead. Show us what you can do, though I shall be very surprised if it's anything at all,' cried the king, giving Hiro Ono a very dark look.

Belinda looked slowly about the palace hall. Standing at the foot of the stairs was a large stone statue of a previous king. Belinda walked silently up to it, gazed at it for a few moments then suddenly,

'Aaaaa-HA!' She gave a great yell, spun round on one foot and launched her other foot at the centre of the statue. There was a splinter of breaking stone and the statue cracked into two separate halves. Even as the top section toppled to the floor, Belinda raised her right arm and sliced the head off with a single blow of her bare hand.

Stormbelly screamed. 'Stop! That's your great-grandfather!' Belinda grinned back and began to walk up the stairway, chopping the thick wooden banisters into little pieces as she did so. Bits of wood cascaded down at the king's feet and came tumbling down the steps.

'Guards!' yelled the king. 'Stop her before she destroys the whole palace!' Up went the guards in hot pursuit, but no sooner did they reach Belinda than she sent them flying with a few well-aimed kicks and blows from her hands. Then she came down to the bottom of the stairs, bowed to her father, bowed to Hiro Ono and her mother and sat down, brushing the dust from her clothes.

Stormbelly sat down too. He collapsed in an armchair. 'Just what have you been teaching my daughter?' he managed to whisper at length.

'The ancient Japanese art of karate,' said Hiro Ono with a little bow.

Stormbelly shook his head. 'I can't believe it. Did she really do that with her bare hands and feet?'

'Of course,' said Hiro Ono. 'But karate is about strength of mind, not of hands and feet. Your wife, who is very wise, explained your daughter's problem to me. Belinda is a very good pupil. She has a very quick brain. Now she can go into the world and you needn't worry.'

'Needn't worry!' cried the king. 'I shall be terrified with her on the loose, smashing up statues and demolishing staircases all over the place.'

Hiro Ono began to explain that it wouldn't be like that at all, but the queen signalled that the king didn't understand and it wasn't worth explaining. She persuaded the king to have an afternoon sleep while they cleared up the hall.

'Well, you've certainly impressed your father, Belinda,' laughed the queen when everything was sorted out. 'Let's hope you can impress a prince!'

2

Belinda's eventful journey

The Princess Belinda was not at all sure that she wanted to impress anybody, least of all a prince. She was quite happy learning karate from Hiro Ono. On the other hand, she was sensible enough to see that she couldn't stay in her father's palace for ever and would have to go out into the wide world sooner or later.

Her chance to find a princely husband came sooner than she expected. King Storm-belly received a letter from a far cousin, King Krust. It was a long letter which made Stormbelly grunt and whistle and humph a lot. That meant it was a thoughtful kind of letter and that Stormbelly had to do some thinking.

What the letter had to say was this. King Krust had heard that Stormbelly had sixteen daughters. He knew that fifteen of them had already married and that their beauty was famed throughout whatever lands they lived in. It so happened that his son, Prince Bruno de Bruno Bunkum Krust, ought to get married and King Krust thought it might be a good idea if Stormbelly's last daughter married him. No doubt she was as beautiful as all the others, and King Krust was prepared to give his son half a kingdom on his marriage.

No wonder Stormbelly humphed a lot. It was an offer he couldn't refuse. The trouble was that Belinda wasn't at all beautiful, even when she wasn't chopping her great-grandfather into little pieces. King Stormbelly thought and thought. He had lots of ideas. Perhaps he could disguise Belinda, dress her up in a lovely dress and put a beautiful blonde wig over her short black hair? Perhaps she could wear a mask, saying that her beauty was so dazzling that she could only remove it at night?

He suggested all this to the queen and she burst out laughing. So did Belinda. That made Stormbelly lose his temper. He kicked two guards, hurt his toes and went to bed for a week. When at last he recovered he took Belinda to one side.

'Belinda, you must at least go and see this prince. He's very handsome and can do sixteen press-ups without stopping. Besides, his father is very rich and half a kingdom is not to be sneezed at.'

Belinda sighed. 'But suppose I don't like him, Father,' she pointed out.

'Goodness me, child! You don't have to *like* him. You only have to marry him.'

Belinda was so surprised she couldn't think of an answer. She went to see Hiro Ono and asked his advice.

'You must go,' he declared. 'You may not find this prince to your liking, but that won't matter. You will find that everything will work out as you wish, Belinda, for if you do not wish it, it will not be so.'

It took Belinda a few minutes to work out what the old Japanese master was saying, but she agreed to go. A few days later she set off, riding in a carriage drawn by four white horses. Hiro Ono and the queen were both sorry to see her go. Belinda promised she would return, and the king said that would be jolly nice, so long as she brought her

husband with her. The carriage set off in a cloud of dust and left the king coughing and spluttering on the doorstep.

The journey was long and tiring. Each night they stopped at a different inn and put up for the night, while the horses rested. Then it was back into the carriage straight after breakfast and jolt, jolt, jolt, all day long.

On the fifth day they ran into trouble. A band of cut-throat robbers came pouring out of the forest, waving their swords and yelling. The horses took fright and bolted. The carriage swayed alarmingly from one side of the track to the other, and poor Belinda was thrown higgledy-piggledy all about inside. First she was on one side, then she was upside-down, then she was under the seat.

Then at last a wheel broke off the rear axle and the horses slipped the traces and took to the hills. The carriage slewed across the path, crashed into a ditch, turned over twice and smashed against a great oak tree. Belinda lay unconscious beneath a pile of carriage cushions and one split suitcase.

With whoops of delight the robbers descended and stripped the broken carriage of everything worth taking. They took the royal jewellery and the royal suitcases. They took the frightened driver's velvet breeches and satin waistcoat. They took all the presents from the Krust royal family. They even took Belinda's beautiful dress and expensive shoes. They rounded up the horses and had quite vanished from sight with them long before Belinda woke up with an aching head.

She crawled out of the broken carriage and stood in her petticoat by the side of it. She looked at the driver and at the mess scattered far and wide by the searching robbers.

'Oh, dear,' she murmured. She helped the poor driver to his feet.

'They were robbers, Your Royalty,' explained the driver, quite unnecessarily. 'I tried to fight them off. I went *biff!* and *baff!* but there were more than I could manage and they took my breeches and my second best waistcoat what your mum gave me last Christmas.'

Belinda soothed his feelings. 'I'm sure you did your best. Now you'd better go back to the palace and tell them what happened. Tell them not to worry. I'm going on to see King Krust. It can't be very far now.' Her keen eyes caught sight of a dusty glitter on the road. She bent down and picked up a gold coin.

'There! Look what those robbers left behind.' Belinda pressed it into the driver's hand. 'You take that. It will get you home safely.'

'Thank you, thank you, Your Royalty. I'll set off right away, I will.' And the driver did just that. Belinda watched his departure and then began walking herself, hoping that she would reach King Krust's palace before she got too hungry.

It was further than she thought. She did not arrive until two days later, by which time she was tired and very hungry. Her petticoat was covered in dust and her skin was smudged with dirt. She did not look at all like a princess.

Certainly the palace guards did not think she was a princess, and they laughed in her face when she told them. It was at this point that Belinda discovered something. Her father was not the only king that King Krust had written to. It seemed he had written hundreds of letters, for the whole town was seething with princesses of every nationality, and all of them had come to win the hand of the fabled Prince Bruno de Bruno Bunkum Krust, for not only was he most wonderfully handsome, but he could do thirty-nine press-ups without stopping. Either he had been practising or somebody was exaggerating.

Now, the Princess Belinda was just a little bit like her father because she had a stubborn streak in her and a hasty temper. When she realized that there were at least three hundred princesses in competition with her, and when the guards just laughed at her, she decided there and then to show them not only that was she a princess but that she'd marry Bruno no matter what.

She looked calmly into the guard's piggy little eyes and said slowly, 'If you do not take me to the king at once, I shall bang your helmet.'

Foolishly the guard just laughed again, so Belinda banged his helmet. Half an hour later when he woke up he discovered that: he had a splitting headache; he couldn't get his helmet off because Belinda had put a very large dent in it; and Belinda had taken herself off to see the king.

It took Belinda a long time to find the king because guards kept trying to stop her. They all refused to believe she was a princess. By the time she reached the king there were forty-six guards with dented helmets lying unconscious all over the palace.

King Krust did not believe her either. He was a very short man, almost as wide as he was tall. He had to stand on a small stool to look at Belinda. He examined her through his monocle.

'You don't look at all like a princess,' he declared. 'You're not even beautiful.'

Belinda thought the king was not exactly

pretty either, but she didn't say so because Hiro Ono had taught her there was little point in making people angry.

Queen Krust was a little kinder than her husband and said that they might at least hear what Belinda had to say. Belinda explained carefully all that had happened to her and why she had turned up in her petticoat looking so filthy. The queen was sympathetic.

'You must have a nice hot bath, my dear, and we'll find you some clean clothes.'

'Just a minute,' butted in the king. 'Suppose she's an impostor?'

'We will give her a little test, to make sure she's a princess,' suggested the queen.

'What sort of test?'

'The usual one. We'll put lots and lots of mattresses on top of each other and put a pea under the bottom one and then see if she can feel it.' The queen turned to Belinda. 'Will that test suit you?'

'I don't mind,' said Belinda.

And so it was arranged.

Belinda felt much better after a hot bath and in clean clothes. When she went to bed she had to climb up a long ladder to reach the top mattress. The king came along to supervise the test and he stood at the bottom of the ladder and stared up at Belinda through a big telescope that his Chief Minister held for him, propped up on his back.

Belinda settled down. The bed was beautifully soft and warm but she squirmed about a bit and wriggled and after five minutes she called down to the king.

'I can't sleep.'

'Why not?' he demanded.

'The mattress is too lumpy.'

King Krust snapped his telescope shut and shrugged. 'Oh well,' he sighed. 'She must be a princess. Never mind.' He strutted out of the room and Belinda turned over, closed her eyes and instantly fell fast asleep, pea or no pea.

3

The royal quest

Belinda nearly had a terrible accident first thing next morning. She woke up feeling wonderful. She felt fresh and lively and cheerful and jumped straight out of bed, quite forgetting that she was perched on top of twenty-seven mattresses and therefore some distance above ground level.

In the nick of time she grabbed at the ladder that had been left at the bedside overnight. The ladder swayed dangerously for a moment as the princess clung to the top rung, with her legs waving wildly beneath her like storm-tossed banners. Then the ladder settled against the mattresses and Belinda clambered down safely.

After breakfast, which she ate with the queen, Belinda set about finding the fabled Prince Bruno de Bruno Bunkum Krust. She was interested to see just what he looked like.

The palace was crawling with princesses, all calling out to their servants in loud, demanding voices. They were all trying terribly hard to impress each other with their beauty and their dresses and their riches.

'Oh, I say,' cried one, 'my daddy owns a whole diamond mine.'

'Really?' screeched another. 'My daddy has two.'

'Never mind, dears,' said a third. 'My daddy has three diamond mines and a golden throne as large as a settee.'

At this point Belinda quietly walked past and said with a lovely smile and bright eyes, 'My daddy has four hundred and thirty-one diamond mines and a golden throne that is so heavy that one side of the palace is quite lop-sided. When we sit down to dinner all the plates and knives and forks all slide to one end of the table and fall off.'

The three princesses were quite flabbergasted, and one of them could not resist asking, 'But, my dear, how do you manage to eat?'

Princess Belinda looked a little sorrowful. 'We have to eat off the floor,' she whispered, as if it were a terrible secret, and she hurried off to look for the prince, leaving the princesses looking quite disgusted.

After Belinda thought she had searched every room in the palace without any success, she at last came to a huge room with giant double doors that had carvings of cherubs all over them. Belinda thought she heard voices on the other side, so she knocked, pushed the doors open and went in. There was the prince.

He was tall and slender and radiantly handsome. His blond hair shone in the sunlight that poured down through the high windows. His face was tanned. His eyes were hazel-brown and they rested on Belinda with a look that made her heart melt. He was sitting with his back straight as a board, shoulders back, in full military uniform – a stunningly handsome sight. Clutched in his slender hands were the reins of his mount – a dusty, stitched-up rocking horse with creaking springs and no tail.

Prince Bruno de Bruno galloped and galloped on his squeaky horse without getting anywhere at all, while just to one side stood a large easel, half covered with clean canvas. Working away with quick, deft charcoal marks was a young painter. He kept stopping and eyeing the galloping prince and then making more marks on his big canvas.

The prince cried out, 'Whoa!' and hastily stopped the rocking horse. The painter put down his charcoal and turned to see what had interrupted them.

'Hallo,' said Belinda cheerfully. Prince Bruno de Bruno tilted his nose towards the ceiling and eyed her distantly.

'Who,' he demanded, 'are you?'

'Princess Belinda.' The prince gave a short snort.

'You! A princess! Hmph, I don't believe you.'

Belinda smiled and shrugged her shoulders. 'Neither did the guards, nor your father, nor your mother for that matter.' The prince ignored all this.

'You're not beautiful enough to be a princess,' he declared.

Meanwhile the royal artist had stepped forward and was quietly watching Belinda. He turned to the prince and pointed out that although Belinda may not look beautiful at first sight, she had extraordinarily blue eyes, and if you looked at the blue eyes for long enough, then you would begin to see that she was truly beautiful.

Again the prince snorted. 'Hubert,' he said, 'you're a fool. Get on with the painting. I want it finished by lunch-time.'

'Yes, Your Highness,' said Hubert the artist, with a short bow, and he returned to his easel and canvas.

Belinda watched the prince for a little longer. She decided he was rather rude, but

no doubt that was because he was a prince. There was certainly no doubt that he was handsome, although she hadn't yet seen him do any press-ups. Besides, if he didn't think very much of her, then she would have to make sure that he changed his mind.

She left the prince, creaking away on his galloping rocking horse, and went off to find a quiet little room for herself, where she could do some thinking and planning. On the way she passed a big hall mirror, and she couldn't resist stopping quickly to take a look at her eyes. Nobody had ever said they were beautiful before. In the mirror they sparkled back at her, but Belinda could not see why they were beautiful at all. She thought they were just like . . . well, like eyes.

In the meantime, King Krust was having a bit of a problem. He was sitting up in bed, surrounded by his most important ministers. The king always held his most important meetings when he was in bed because his ministers made such long speeches he kept dropping off to sleep. If you're going to drop off to sleep, he pointed out, you may as well be in bed and do it properly.

'We've got a problem,' he announced.

'Yes, Your Majesty.'

'To put it another way, we've got four hundred and three problems, because that's how many princesses there are. They're cluttering up the palace and eating me out of house and home.'

'Yes, Your Majesty,' nodded the old and important ministers.

'Well, what are we going to do about it?' the king snapped.

A chorus of ums and ahs filled the royal bedchamber. One minister pressed his fingertips together one by one and coughed.

'I suppose we could poison them,' he said.

'That's a good idea. That would get rid of them,' said the others.

King Krust sighed. 'It is not a good idea at all. What do you think would happen when their fathers found out? They'd all be coming round here, waving their swords and things. No, no. We can't have that.'

There was a long silence, during which the king began to snore. He jerked awake. 'The whole point is,' he grunted, 'we are trying to find a wife for my son. How on earth do we choose the right wife out of all that lot?'

'Perhaps we could give them numbers and draw one out of a hat?'

'Don't be so stupid!' he snapped, seizing his crown and holding it out for all to see. 'How can you put numbers in that? They'd go straight through!'

The other important ministers glared at

the unlucky one who had made the suggestion. 'How stupid!' they grumbled. Then another one had a good idea.

'Your Majesty, suppose we gave all the princesses a task to complete. Then whoever did it first could marry your son.'

At first there was no reply because King Krust was fast asleep again. The poor minister had to repeat his suggestion all over again.

'Hmmm,' mumbled the king. 'That might work. What sort of task?'

'Well, I need some buttons sewn on my shirt,' one suggested.

'My lawn needs mowing,' said another.

'I say, I left my poor wife with her big toe stuck in the bath tap. I don't know how she's going to get it out.'

'Saw her leg off!' cried the king, standing up in his bed and waving his little arms about. 'This is ridiculous. They should be fighting dragons or something, not sewing on buttons and pulling toes out of bath taps.'

'Yes, Your Majesty, but we don't have any dragons.'

One of the more silent ministers mumbled something about his wife being rather fierce, but nobody heard him.

'We must have something dangerous somewhere in the kingdom,' said the king, sitting down again.

'Your Majesty, I believe we do have a Bogle somewhere. Hiding in the Marsh at the End of the World, I think.'

'My goodness, that's a long way off. That's probably why I've never heard of it before. What on earth is a Bogle?' King Krust snuggled down under the bedcovers as if he expected a bedtime story.

'Bogles are a bit like men,' explained the important minister. 'But they are very hairy and have long arms, long fingers and even longer fingernails.'

'Ugh,' said the king.

'Quite so, Your Majesty. Their eyes glow in the dark, and they have hair sprouting out of their nostrils and ears. They are not very pretty,' added the minister, quite unnecessarily.

'No, well, I wasn't thinking of inviting him to my birthday party, you know. Tell me what they eat.'

'Slugs and beetles, Your Majesty, but if they could, they would eat humans. Every so often they come out of the marsh and seize a few people. They're never ever heard of again.'

King Krust clapped his hands. 'Just the job,' he said. 'He'll do nicely. Has he got a name, this Bogle?'

'I believe he's known as Knackerleevee.'

'Good, good, good,' said the king, jumping out of bed. 'Get the princesses together and I shall be down shortly.'

It took the king three hours to get himself dressed, partly because he couldn't be bothered to undo his cuff buttons and consequently his arms got stuck in his shirt sleeves. When at last he arrived in the main hall he found it jam-packed with the princesses. The noise was awful.

A big gong sounded, and King Krust raised his arms.

'Silence, silence!' he yelled. 'I have an announcement. Now, you have all come here to marry my wonderful son, Prince

Bruno de Bruno Bunkum Krust.' Here there were great cheers and a curtain was pulled back to reveal the portrait that Belinda had seen earlier that morning. The paint was still wet, but there for all to see was Bruno de Bruno, dashing across the countryside on a magnificent white horse. Belinda, who was crushed right at the back of the hall, couldn't help thinking it was a shame that nobody else had seen the stitched-up rocking horse.

Several princesses swooned at the sight of the handsome prince and had to be carried from the room, to be dumped in a passage outside. The king continued.

'Now, there are far too many princesses to marry my son – that honour can fall to only one of you. I have therefore arranged for a competition. Whoever completes this task will marry my son and receive half my kingdom . . . but not the bit with the diamond mine. I'm having that half. At the far corner of my kingdom, in the Marsh at the End of the World, there lives a Bogle. His name is Knackerleevee. He is very hairy, smells of fish and eats people. I want him brought back, dead or alive.'

At this announcement a whole lot more of the princesses swooned away at the thought of smelly fish. Another couple of hundred took to their heels and ran out of the palace,

never to be seen again. In short, only two princesses were left, standing all alone in the big hall.

The king could hardly believe his eyes. It was wonderful. All the princesses had gone at last. He stared down at the two left behind.

'I know you,' he said to Belinda, 'but who are you?'

The second princess, who was, naturally, astonishingly beautiful, stepped forward and gave the king a dazzling smile.

'Your Majesty,' she crooned. 'I am the Princess Saramanda Sneak, and I shall bring you the Bogle dead or alive, just as you wish.'

The princess bent over his hand and gave it a sloppy kiss. King Krust turned to his important ministers with a beaming face.

'There,' he said. 'I think that was an excellent idea of mine!' And he added in a loud whisper that Belinda heard quite clearly, 'I do hope Saramanda wins. Isn't she a stunner? I don't fancy that other one as a daughter-in-law at all.'

4

Princess Saramanda Sneak

Belinda was eager to start off straight away for the Marsh at the End of the World, but King Krust was in no particular hurry.

'You may as well stay for tea,' he said. 'And then it will be too late to start before nightfall, so you may as well spend the night here and set off in the morning.'

The truth of the matter was that he liked looking at Princess Saramanda. After all, she was a rather stunning creature, with sparkling gold hair that flowed right down to her waist. It glittered with tiny gems.

The queen wasn't too pleased to see her husband staring at this new princess.

'I don't think that Salamander girl is very nice,' she said, in private, to her husband.

'Not Salamander dear, Saramanda. A salamander is a kind of blotchy lizard, I think.'

'Exactly. I don't trust lizards and I don't trust her either.'

King Krust began to waddle quickly round and round the room.

'And I don't think much of that Belinda person either. She comes here in her petticoat with mud all over her face. She uses our dresses and sleeps in our beds, not to mention half killing the guards. Do you know that most of them are still in hospital? I mean to say, what kind of princess goes around clonking guards on the head?'

The queen shrugged. 'Quite honestly I have often felt like doing that myself,' and she gave her husband a withering look which he pretended he hadn't seen.

In fact, the queen was quite right to mistrust the Princess Saramanda, even if she did so for the wrong reasons. The princess was very pretty to look at, but inside her pretty head was a very mean brain. Saramanda was constantly dreaming up wicked plots. At the age of three she cheated her two older brothers out of their dinners for a whole week. By the time she was eleven she had caused a war between her father's kingdom and their neighbour's, by kidnapping the neighbour's favourite poodle and refusing to return it until a large ransom had been paid.

Saramanda wished to marry Bruno de Bruno more than anything else in the world. She realized that when King Krust died, his son would inherit the rest of the kingdom anyway, and then she would be queen and she would have the half with the diamond mine too. Saramanda was very fond of diamonds and would do anything to get her slender fingers on them. She even employed her own band of robbers who went about the countryside taking diamonds from anybody who had them. But, being robbers, they took everything else as well. They handed the diamonds over to the princess and kept the rest for themselves. These were the robbers who had stolen Belinda's things on her way to King Krust's castle.

That night Princess Saramanda slept very well, dreaming up different ways of getting rid of Belinda and winning Bruno de Bruno – such a handsome chap too. She adored tall, strong men with big shoulders and blond hair. No doubt he would shower her with diamonds.

The following morning King Krust came to the palace gateway to see the two princesses off. A grand assembly of important people had gathered around the prancing horses. Belinda and Saramanda eyed each other. Then the royal painter came along, sitting in a small cart loaded high with canvas and easels and pots and pots of paint.

'He's going too,' explained the king. 'I want a nice picture of the battle for the Great Hall. There's a horrible splodge on the wall

where the queen threw her rice pudding at me last year, and I've been wondering how to cover it up. A big picture of a Bogle Battle will do me nicely.' The king turned to the royal artist. 'Make sure there's lots of blood and everything in it, Hubert.'

'Yes, Your Majesty.'

Princess Saramanda smiled sweetly down from her horse. 'I do hope it's not our blood, Your Majesty!'

He widened his eyes. 'Oh, my goodness, no. At least, not your blood, you little fairy cloud!'

These words did not give Belinda much hope, but at that moment she caught sight of Prince Bruno de Bruno, standing alone on a high balcony and watching them. The wind fluttered through his golden locks and he stared down at them with his hazel eyes, his strong jaw jutting out as proud as a ship cleaving the waves.

She turned her lively horse, waved good-bye and cantered away towards the Marsh at the End of the World. Hubert the painter gave his old horse a prod with a paint brush, and the cart rumbled after her.

Princess Saramanda watched them both go, a smile on her lips.

'Keep going, dear Belinda!' she whispered to herself. 'I've arranged a little party for you – a party of robbers. With a bit of luck that royal painter might meet with an unfortunate accident too.' So saying, she blew a kiss at the king, who immediately turned bright red and almost fell off his royal stool. She then rode slowly after Belinda and Hubert.

It was a lovely day. The sun was splendid above, and the clear sky matched the brilliance of Belinda's eyes – not that she realized that, of course, as she trotted cheerfully through the woods and fields.

Not far behind came Hubert, humming softly to himself and trying to decide if Belinda's eyes should be cobalt blue or cyan. 'Cobalt is too blue,' he said to himself. 'And cyan is a shade too light, so I shall mix them both together and that should be about right.

I'll call it Belinda blue.' This thought seemed to make him even happier and he began to sing in a loud, strong voice. The old horse joined in too, and they made so much noise together that at first they didn't hear the shouts and bangs and yells that were coming from the wood just ahead.

Saramanda's robbers had decided it was time to swoop down on poor Belinda. Saramanda had said they could do what they liked with her. Perhaps they might like to ransom her, or if they couldn't be bothered with all that trouble, they might prefer to kill her – if they got the chance!

As soon as Belinda saw the twenty or so robbers hurtling down the hillside towards her, she realized they were the very same robbers who had robbed her once before. She pulled in her horse sharply and jumped lightly to the ground. She tied her horse safely to a tree and then stood in a large clearing where the robbers could see her quite plainly.

'I'm getting fed up with this,' she muttered. 'Wherever I go there's trouble. I wish Hiro Ono was with me. Never mind, there are only about twenty of them.'

By this time the robbers were pounding through the trees, whooping and shouting and waving great curved swords over their heads. One of them managed to chop the feather off his own hat, he was so excited. They circled round Princess Belinda, laughing away like the jolly robbers they were.

'What shall we do with her, mateys?' cried their leader, a big fat robber with a black beard like sofa-stuffing.

'Chop off her head!'

'Chop off her legs!'

And they all began to chant.

'Chip, chop, chop off her legs! Chip, chop, chop off her head!'

They got down from their horses and poked their swords at Belinda and marched round and round, still chanting away. Belinda stood quite still and calmly watched each one.

Hubert the painter had heard all the singing, and he drove his cart into the woods to see what was going on. He was horrified. There was poor little Belinda, surrounded by nasty robbers. Hubert felt helpless. 'I'm helpless Hubert,' he thought. He wanted to cover his eyes, for he hardly dared to look. But if he didn't look, he wouldn't know what was going to happen. So he covered his eyes and parted his fingers so he could see between them.

He saw the big, fat chief robber rush up to

Belinda with his flashing sword. A moment later the sword lay in two pieces and the robber chief was stuck in a tree, trying to get his breath back. Hubert rubbed his eyes in disbelief. Then two more robbers rushed furiously upon little Belinda. She spun on one heel, knocked one senseless with a flying kick to the jaw and crammed the other's helmet so far down on his head that his skull came poking out of the top. He staggered off among the trees.

The robbers realized that Belinda was no ordinary princess. They banded together in a big bunch and then charged at her, snarling and snapping like mad dogs. For several seconds Hubert could not see what was happening. Everybody was rushing hither and thither. Dust clouds burst all around the skirmishing robbers, and the yells and bangs and clangs were enough to deafen a snake. Since snakes don't have ears, you can imagine how loud it all was.

Hubert crouched behind his tree and watched. First one robber came flying out of the cloud of dust and landed in a still heap, then two more staggered out, clutching their stomachs and holding each other up. Another robber went hurtling up into a tree and landed alongside the robber chief. A fifth robber came spinning out of the fight like some gigantic flying starfish. He hit a tree trunk and sank to the ground.

Suddenly it was all over. The remaining robbers dashed to their horses and disappeared, yelping, over the horizon. As the dust settled, Hubert at last saw Princess Belinda. She was brushing a smudge of dirt off one shoulder.

'Oh, look,' she said to Hubert as he came creeping up to her in utter amazement, 'I've got some dirt on this dress and it's not even mine.'

Hubert was speechless. He pointed in silence at the groaning robbers all about them. 'How did you do it?' he croaked. Belinda laughed and took a step closer.

'I'll show you, shall I?'

Hubert almost jumped out of his skin.

'No, no. It's quite all right. It was wonderful. I've never seen anything like it.'

There was a sound of approaching hooves and the Princess Saramanda trotted into sight. Her face turned white at the spectacle of half her robbers lying bruised and broken on the ground – not to mention the two stuck up a tree.

Hubert rushed eagerly to Saramanda and told her all that he had seen. Princess Saramanda was seething with fury inside, but she smiled sweetly at Belinda and said in her oh-so-soft voice, 'My, my, you have got a temper, haven't you? Well, see you at the Marsh at the End of the World!' And she rode on. Saramanda was not furious for long. A rather nice thought came into her head. She had been wondering all along how to catch the Bogle and now she knew what to do.

'I'll let that dear little muscle-bag Belinda catch him. She can do all the hard work and I shall do the easy bit – taking the Bogle back to the castle and marrying Bruno!'

5

The Bogle

The Marsh at the End of the World was the most dismal place that Princess Belinda had ever seen. Swirling mists drifted over grey tussocks of dirty grass. Dark pools of stagnant, scummy water were pimpled with bubbles. They would slowly grow until they at last burst with a muffled *plop!* and a nauseating stink would fill the air.

Belinda stood on the edge, with the mud seeping over her shoes. She peered anxiously into the mist. Hubert left the heavy cart at a safe distance, then came sloping over.

'It's not very pretty, is it?' he said mournfully. 'I don't know what King Krust will think if I paint a picture of this. It's all dirty grey and green – and the smell is terrible.'

Belinda smiled and looked at the royal painter, who was busily smothering his sensitive nose with a large, grubby handkerchief.

'You can't paint a smell,' she said.

'I thought I'd be able to paint some nice

48

landscapes,' complained Hubert. 'Views of shining mountains and trees waving in the wind. I hate painting people, especially King Krust. He just gets fatter, and the queen always complains that I've made her nose too large. I'm much better at landscapes, you know. But this – it's just green: grey-green, dark green, grass-green, mid-green, green, green and more green. It's utterly, greenly boring.' The painter heaved a sigh and plodded back to the cart to unload his materials.

Belinda was glad to be left alone. She was nervous. She did not know what might be out in the marsh, lurking, ready to pounce. She knew only that she had to enter the mist and the mire and find the Bogle. Princess Saramanda might already be in there.

Belinda tried not to think of her fears as she plunged resolutely into the marsh. Soon her feet were sinking down into the oozing mud, and sometimes she sank right up to the waist. She tried to keep near the big mounds of grass and managed to pull herself out by hauling on the thick grass.

There was the stench too, as she disturbed all the old, stagnant pools. It was very unpleasant, but could not be avoided. She was covered with the foul-smelling mud and looked as if a wet and sloppy cow field had

suddenly exploded as she was walking through it.

At length she came to a halt. She climbed on to a big mound of grass and stood there, panting, shivering and lost. Around her the mist slowly ribboned out across the marsh. Not a sound was to be heard, except the slow plopping of the bubbles of gas. Nor was there anything to be seen save the grey-green wasteland stretching in every direction.

The chill of the marsh-water seeped into Belinda's bones, and a horrid fear began to creep into her heart. She cupped her hands to her mouth.

'Knackerleevee! Knackerleevee!' Her voice died away on the marsh wind. A bubble rose and burst and Belinda held her nose.

'Knackerleevee! Bogle! I am the Princess

Belinda and have come to fight you. You Bogle-buffoon!'

Again there was silence. Belinda peered through the mists. Sometimes she thought she saw a huddled shape moving, then it would vanish. The silence was sinister. She cupped her hands once more, then heard it – a faint splashing, far away at the back of the marsh. 'Knackerleevee!' she yelled. 'I'm over here, you great oaf!'

The splashes came nearer and a grumbling, raspy old voice drifted through the mist. 'Great oaf, am I? Bogle-buffoon? What kind of fool would call Knackerleevee a buffoon? It must be a king-sized, cross-eyed fool!' A grey, hunched shape began to appear through the mist, plunging carelessly through the puddles. 'And fools always make very good sandwiches,' the Bogle went on, talking mostly to himself now.

He came nearer and nearer, grunting softly as he plodded towards Belinda. Her serene sky-blue eyes grew larger and rounder as she began to make out his truly huge shape, moving through the mists like some monstrous human dinosaur. A chill fear numbed her brain and froze her muscles.

Out of the mist came Knackerleevee, his small eyes glowing a nasty pink-red colour. His wide, flared nostrils quivered with clumps of black hair. His chest was swaddled with muscle and so much wiry hair that he resembled a walking doormat. The Bogle stopped a few paces away from the princess and began to smile. It was a slow smile that ended up showing all his teeth – big, black and sharp.

'I'm Knackerleevee,' he growled. 'And I eat princesses for my tea, when I can find them.' An expression of disgust twisted his long and crooked mouth into an ugly knot. He rolled his red eyes and smashed one hairy fist into a pool. Brown water sprayed into the air. 'I don't see much point in eating you! You're too skinny, and I dare say you taste of jasmine perfume.' The Bogle spat loudly into the marsh. 'The last princess I ate tasted of jasmine perfume. She tasted foul, but at least she had a bit of meat on her!' He reached out with surprising speed and felt Belinda's left arm. 'Ugh – it's like string. Why don't they make fat princesses any more?' And Knackerleevee grunted and snorted, picked his nose and glared steadily at Belinda with his little red eyes.

Now, Belinda's heart was thumping away like one of those road-flatteners, but Hiro Ono had taught her well. 'Always stay calm,' he had told her. 'There is nothing that frightens the enemy more than calmness.

53

Muscles and weapons are nothing so long as you show no fear.' So although her insides were running away into every possible corner to hide, outwardly Belinda appeared calm and untroubled.

'Well,' she said, 'as a matter of fact I haven't come here so that you can eat me. I've come to defeat you in battle.'

Knackerleevee banged his fists on his knees and then on his head – which made his eyes water quite a lot – and roared with laughter. 'You couldn't fight me!' he yelled. 'You're just a skinny girl. Princesses don't fight!' He thrust his face up against hers and growled. 'They get eaten! I could break you into so many pieces it would take a year to find them all. I could throw you so far you'd probably never even land anywhere. You fight me? Ha!'

Princess Belinda began to redden. She was getting fed up with all this nonsense. She angrily dragged an old log from the marsh and stuck it upright in front of her. It was as thick as one of Knackerleevee's legs. The Bogle narrowed his eyes and rasped, 'Now what are you trying to do?'

Belinda took a deep breath and concentrated. 'Haaaaaa – akk!' Her fist sliced the air. There was a dull *crack!* and the top half of the log toppled over and fell with a splash into the marsh. Belinda straightened up, glanced quietly at the Bogle and bowed.

Knackerleevee stuck out his bottom lip and dribbled thoughtfully. Then he grunted down his nose and pulled another thick log from the marsh and set it upright. He glared nastily at Belinda and then at the log and cried out,

'Urrrr – UNK!' He smashed his fist into the log and leapt away screaming, 'Owwwwowowowooooooarhowow,' with his fist jammed under his other arm and hopping from one leg to the other.

'It took me a long time to learn how to do that,' said Belinda gravely. 'You should never try such things without proper training.'

The Bogle sank down on to a mound and nursed his fist. He was broken and dejected. His jaw drooped on to his chest, and he regarded Belinda with such pale and sorrowful eyes that if she wasn't sure he was a big, brave Bogle, she would have thought he was crying.

'It can't be,' he moaned. 'I eat princesses . . .' He glanced up at Belinda. 'I *used* to eat princesses. How did you do it? Such strength from such a little person.'

'It's called karate, and it took me seven years to learn.' Belinda paused and studied the dejected creature in front of her. 'Look, does this mean that you're not even going to fight me?'

Knackerleevee recoiled in horror. 'Fight you! No, never!' He suddenly threw himself at Belinda's feet in a muddy huddle. 'No, princess! Don't fight me, but teach me karate! Teach me how to do that thing with the log.'

Belinda's insides had stopped running away to hide and were rushing back to their proper places, giggling madly. Outwardly she remained calm – it wouldn't do for a princess to giggle in front of a Bogle.

'Teach me karate, Your High Royalship,' pleaded Knackerleevee.

'You'll have to come with me,' said Belinda sharply.

'I will, I will.'

'Wherever I go?'

'Wherever you go, Royalness. I shall follow you everywhere if only you will teach me the secret of your strength.'

Belinda reached down and touched the Bogle for the first time. His skin was hairy and caked with mud, but it was warm and soft underneath. 'I don't think you're such a bad beast after all,' she said. The Bogle gazed up at her with grateful eyes.

'Everybody's got to eat something,' he pointed out.

'Hmmm. I think eating people is a bit much, you know.'

'But they taste so nice, Princess! Especially the legs!'

'Even when they're like string?' suggested Belinda. Knackerleevee lowered his eyes, mortified.

'I'm sorry I was so rude,' he stammered.

'Oh, come on, you big lump! Stop being so gloomy. Get up and show me the way out of this horrible place.'

Knackerleevee dragged himself out of the mud. He swung Belinda up on to his shoulders to ride in triumph, and together they set off for dry land.

'We must find Hubert,' hiccuped Belinda, who was getting rather bounced about on the Bogle's massive shoulders.

'Who's Hubert, Your Royalshipness?' asked the Bogle, splashing through the marsh.

'He's an artist, and he's rather sensitive, so try not to upset him. Oh, and Knacker-leevee?'

'Yes, O Royalshipnesty?'

'My name is Belinda, and if you call me a royal whatsit once more, I shall give you a demonstration of karate on your head. Do you understand?'

The Bogle grinned and plunged on

through the mist. He began to sing in a cheese-grater voice, and soon the swirling mists drew apart and they struggled out on to dry land. The sun was shining, the marsh was behind them and there was Hubert, sitting behind a large canvas with a big brushful of grey-green paint at the ready.

The royal painter looked so terrified you might well have thought he'd seen a Bogle beasty, which he had, so no wonder. But Belinda climbed down from the Bogle's back and told Hubert the whole story, and at the end they even shook hands. Hubert was still holding his big paintbrush, which was rather unfortunate for Knackerleevee, but he said he didn't mind since he was practically that colour anyway.

They were just thinking of sitting down and opening the packed lunches they'd brought on the cart when there was a cheerful shout from a nearby rock and the Princess Saramanda popped up her pretty head, all a-glitter with diamonds.

'Yoohoo!' she cried ever so sweetly. 'Belinda! Look behind you!'

Belinda glanced over her shoulder. 'Oh dear,' she murmured.

Waiting behind them, and armed to the teeth with swords and bows and real guns that went *bang!* if you pulled the triggers, were Saramanda's cut-throat robbers. There were only nine of them, as the others were still in hospital, and some of the nine had their arms in slings or were propped up on crutches.

Nevertheless they were there, and they would not come any closer. They pointed their guns with a great deal of menace while Saramanda explained the situation.

'Really, Belinda, it is most terribly kind of you to get this ugly Bogle beasty for me. King Krust is going to be *so* delighted. Do you know, he'll probably be so pleased he'll let me marry that deliciously handsome Bruno creature and then I shall have half a kingdom too.'

Saramanda fluttered her long eyelashes and sighed at the thought of it all. 'Now my cut-throat robbers, take this smelly mattress on legs and tie him to the cart. When you've done that you can take these two back into the marsh – and make sure they never come out!'

6

Hubert is artful

Belinda watched helplessly while Knacker-leevee was forced to the old cart. The wary robbers kept their distance. They had learnt their lesson and they knew that if they came too close to either the Bogle or Belinda there would be trouble. So they stayed safely a few paces away, waving their swords and guns.

Belinda felt very sorry for Knackerleevee. Things had taken quite an unexpected turn, and there was no telling what would happen to the Bogle when Saramanda turned up at the castle. She watched sadly as the cart jerked forwards and slowly rumbled away down the track and out of sight, with the Bogle bound and gagged and stuffed beneath some old canvases of Hubert's.

Belinda and Hubert had their own problems, for the nine remaining robbers were obviously looking forward to carrying out Saramanda's orders. The new leader (you will remember that the old one was left stuck up a tree) was a fine fellow, a good five feet tall and wearing a black hat with a rim so enormous you could have filled it with water and sailed little boats round it. He also wore big black boots and he kept his swords, any number of them, stuffed down the insides. If he took his boots off, you would have seen his feet were covered in plasters.

The other robbers were all grinning madly and wriggling their swords and guns and muttering dark threats.

'Chop off their heads!'

'No – chop off their ears!'

'Chop everything. Chip, chop, chop the lot!'

Belinda had heard it all before, but last time she had been able to save herself with a display of karate. It didn't seem as if she would have the chance this time and she was quite at a loss to know what to do. She whispered to Hubert beside her.

'I'm sorry for getting you into this mess.'

Hubert stared glumly at his unfinished painting of Belinda fighting the Bogle. He wished that he could do something for once, but all he could do was paint pictures of kings and important people. He couldn't fight, not even to save his life. He wasn't at all brave. Sometimes the royal painter hated himself.

The robber chief swaggered up to Belinda and stuck a knife under her chin. 'Come on,

Your Most Royal Royal Highness. We've got to take a little walk. This way!'

Hubert suddenly jumped forward and grabbed the robber's arm. 'Stop a moment. Hold it . . . That's it! Fantastic!' The robber chief half closed one eye and glared at Hubert.

'What are you playing at?' he growled.

The royal painter slowly shook his head and murmured, 'Such a fine head! When you moved just now you looked so strong and powerful. It really should be painted.' Hubert stroked the robber chief's bristly beard. 'Magnificent. Think how it would look on canvas, with a big gold frame round it. Such a head!'

By this time the robber chief was looking considerably less angry and was preening his beard thoughtfully. 'Of course I look magnificent,' he declared. 'I'm a cut-throat robber chief.'

Hubert clasped his hands together. 'Please,' he began, 'please let me paint your portrait before I die. I've always wanted to paint a picture of somebody marvellous, somebody whose face really shows strength of character and brave resolve. You have just that face . . .'

Two of the other robbers pushed Hubert roughly to one side.

'If he's going to paint you, then he's going to paint all of us. We'll all have our picture painted, won't we, lads?'

'Oh yes!' cried Belinda. 'Do paint them all, Hubert. They're such a fine-looking bunch of fellows.'

Now all the robbers began to lick their fingers and tidy their hair. They brushed the dry mud from their breeches and tucked their shirts in. Hubert began to organize them into a little group. The robber chief was still mighty suspicious, but he was desperate to have his portrait done by a real, royal artist. He stood very stiff and pompous in the middle of his gang and pointed his gun at Princess Belinda.

'Don't you get any funny ideas, Princess, or this gun will go off and you'll go off with it.'

Belinda smiled and replied, 'I wouldn't dream of it.' And she winked at Hubert. The painter set up his easel and canvas and selected his paints. Then he began to paint. He worked quickly, slapping the colours on and working them deftly with master-strokes of the brush. The robbers began to shift about nervously, dying to know what their picture looked like. Hubert threw the brush over his shoulder.

'Finished!' he cried. There was a mad

charge as the robbers dashed round to the other side of the easel to see their portrait. Hubert carefully withdrew.

There was a great roar of laughter, and another one of rage. 'Ha, ha! Look at the chief's ear. It looks like a cabbage.'

'It *is* a cabbage. It is a cabbage, and look at his nose. It's all purple and blue. And look, look, that's you at the back there.'

'Where? That's not me.'

'Of course it is. Your nose looks just like that cucumber!'

'My nose isn't like a cucumber. That's you – don't you even recognize yourself? If you don't recognize the nose, you can tell by those crossed eyes. I've never seen anybody as cross-eyed as you in my life.'

'Me cross-eyed! Who are you calling cross-eyed, you mouldy cucumber snout? I'll make you cross-eyed!' Out came the swords and soon the nine cut-throat robbers were hard at it, slicing each other up and poking and prodding and biffing and baffing until there was so much dust they would never have seen Belinda and Hubert slowly creep away even if they had stopped for a moment.

The princess and the painter found the robbers' horses tied to some nearby trees. Belinda jumped up into the saddle and called to Hubert.

'Come on, hurry!'

'I can't ride. I've never ridden a horse in all my life.'

Belinda pulled her mount round and rode to Hubert. 'It's very easy,' she explained. 'You sit on its back and put one leg on each side and hold on tight.'

'I know that!' snapped Hubert. 'I'm not stupid. How do I get up on to it?'

'You think about nine robbers about to stick their swords into you and jump!'

Hardly were the words out of her mouth than Hubert was up on a horse, wobbling a little and facing the tail, but still in the saddle. Belinda held the horse steady while Hubert turned himself round. Then she released all the other horses and shooed them away, so that they went off at a gallop, leaving the robbers with a transport problem.

Hubert and Belinda then set off at a gallop themselves, determined to catch up with the cheating Saramanda before she reached the palace and claimed both prince and half the kingdom for herself. Hubert had a very hard time of it and he felt as if he were trying to control a high-speed earthquake. He was so shaken and jarred he was quite certain that by the time he reached the palace all his bones would be lying in tiny fragments at the bottom of his boots and the palace guards would have to tip him out on to the floor when he arrived.

Everything seemed to do its best to slow them down. First of all Hubert forgot to hold on to his reins and did a wonderful backward somersault over the horse's tail to land in the hard dust. Then he forgot to press his knees against the horse's sides and bounced so high he landed almost on the horse's head – and the horse wasn't at all pleased about that. Then they went galloping through a wood and no fewer than five tree branches whopped the poor painter in the stomach or on the head and knocked him flying from his panting mount.

At last Belinda gave up and declared that he would have to sit behind her and hold on tight. By this time Hubert was only semi-conscious, and it was the only thing he was capable of doing anyway.

With the extra weight they could not make much speed, and they had to stop frequently

to let the poor horse regain some strength. Eventually they trotted up a long rise, and when they reached the top they saw King Krust's castle in front of them, on the far side of the plain.

Belinda could just make out a puff of dust crawling towards the great castle wall. Even as she watched, the distant cart stopped at the gates.

'Well,' muttered Belinda, 'she's got there before us. But I'm not giving up yet.' She urged the horse down the hill towards the glittering castle.

7

A princely prize

Princess Saramanda Sneak entered the castle in triumph. King Krust himself came hurrying down the castle's great stairway, almost tripping over his real fox-fur robe in his rush to greet the princess. She waited at the bottom of the stairs, her eyes bright with success and her heart black with cheating.

The king had to stand on the bottom step to say hallo, and even then Saramanda was taller than he was.

'You were so quick!' cried King Krust. Then he spied the red paint on her dress. 'Are you hurt? Are you wounded? Are you all right?'

The princess gave a little shrug. 'It's nothing. Just a flesh wound. The Bogle must have scratched me as I threw him over my shoulder.'

The king's eyes rolled right round and back to where they started. 'You threw the Bogle over your shoulder? Goodness, such strength. Bruno will be delighted.' The king gave her a sly grin. 'He's been practising, you know.'

At that moment Prince Bruno de Bruno Bunkum Krust himself made a guest appearance. He stood at the top of the stairs, his firm jaw jutting out firmly, his shoulders bulging with overworked muscles beneath his dapper tunic and his half-closed eyes resting lazily on the company below.

Most of the ladies-in-waiting swooned at the mere sight of so handsome a creature. He came slowly down the stairs, his sword clinking at his side, until he finally reached the bottom step and stood in front of the Princess Saramanda, eyeing her carefully.

'Ah,' he drawled. 'So you are Saramanda. My father has told me all about you. He is quite right. You're very beautiful. I hear you threw the Bogle over your shoulder.'

The princess smiled sweetly and curtsied. 'Yes,' and she blushed prettily and added, 'I'm afraid my dress got a little blood on it.'

The prince studied the paint stains gravely. 'Indeed. You must find a lady-in-waiting and have it seen to. Then we shall discuss the wedding.' Bruno leant forward and took Saramanda's hand and kissed it.

'Just a minute, just a minute,' interrupted

the king. 'We haven't even seen this Bogle yet. Where is this horrible monster? Is it dead or alive?'

'I have it in the cart, Your Majesty.'

'Oh, fine fine. Bring in the cart!' roared King Krust. The huge doors were pushed open and Hubert's old cart was rolled into the hall. 'Isn't that Hubert's cart?' asked the king. 'I wonder what happened to him.'

Saramanda bent close to the king's ear and whispered. 'I'm afraid he was rather frightened by all the roaring and he ran away. I don't know where he went.'

King Krust patted her hand. 'Don't worry, my dear. Plenty more royal painters where he came from. Never did like him much. He always painted the queen's nose too large and made me sit quite still for hours, you know. Hours and hours. I used to get pins and needles in my erhum, you know, my . . .'

'Oh yes!' cried Saramanda. 'I know.' The king nodded with great seriousness.

Then the old canvas cover was pulled from the cart and there was Knackerleevee, peacefully snoring away at the bottom of the cart with his legs tied to his arms and his arms tied to his legs. In fact, there was so much rope and hair he looked like a giant ball of wool, very badly wound.

Everybody gathered round and stared at the famous monster from the Marsh at the End of the World. King Krust borrowed a guard's spear and gave the Bogle a little poke. 'Are you sure it's alive?' he asked the princess.

Bruno de Bruno was holding his nose and waving one hand in front of his face. 'I say, it's a bit of a strong pong, isn't it?'

Somebody suggested that the Bogle looked like a mouldy old carpet and smelled like one too. Everybody began to lean forward and poke the helpless creature, and eventually Knackerleevee must have begun to feel something through his thick hide because he opened one pink eye and glared out through the sides of the cart. Then he snorted and tried to stretch himself. Finding himself all bound up, he suddenly remembered what had befallen him.

Now, Knackerleevee may have been ugly and dirty and smelly and not too clever, but he was proud. So he didn't lose his temper or

growl or roar and spit. He just lowered his head once more and stared back at all the people staring at him.

King Krust was disappointed. 'It doesn't look very fierce,' he ventured.

'That's because I tied him up,' said Saramanda. The Bogle watched the princess thoughtfully, thinking that she was the one who had caused all the trouble.

'Was it a terrible fight?' asked Bruno, peering closely at Knackerleevee's long fingernails.

'He was very strong,' said Saramanda,

leaning against the cart. 'But I beat him in the end,' and she smiled.

The Bogle suddenly heaved himself up-right, with a roaring splutter that was half laughter and half anger. 'That daisy-faced-little-bitty-pretty-pretty princess! Beat me? She couldn't squeeze a lemon! Do you think she fought me? Is that what she's told you? I'll tell you what . . .'

But King Krust had got his spear and poked it angrily at the Bogle. The king's face was quite red. 'How dare you speak like that to a princess! Don't you dare to call her

daisy-faced – or she'll throw you over her shoulder again.'

'Ha! She couldn't throw a banana skin, let alone me. I'm Knackerleevee the Bogle, and nobody, nobody, gets the better of me except . . .'

'Don't listen to him,' cried Saramanda. 'He's just being nasty because he lost the fight.'

Knackerleevee gave a low growl and tried to get away from the little pin pricks of the king's spear. 'It was Belinda who beat me, and I don't mind telling you. She's the strongest and the kindest person I have ever met. As for this glittering thing here – she's a cheat and a liar.'

Prince Bruno de Bruno rushed up to the cart and rattled the sides furiously. 'Don't you dare speak to my future wife like that, you overgrown fungus. Apologize at once!'

Knackerleevee glared at the prince with his pink eyes and snorted. 'Go away and do your press-ups, you overgrown muscle.'

Then everybody began to speak and shout and yell at once. The hall was in uproar, and in the midst of it all there was a clatter of hooves and Belinda and Hubert came riding right into the hall. Princess Belinda gave a cry of delight as she spotted the Bogle.

'Knackerleevee! You're all right! Oh, I am glad.'

'Guards, surround that princess!' yelled Bruno de Bruno, quite white with fury. There was a clatter of armour and the guards rushed up and around Belinda's prancing horse.

She gazed calmly down at them. 'I think I can guess what's been happening,' she mused. 'Saramanda has told you her story.'

The prince stiffened. 'Quite right, and I intend to marry her in the morning!'

Belinda looked at Knackerleevee and the king waving his spear about as if he were the bravest king in the world. She saw the demure Saramanda with her sweet, innocent smile, and she saw Bruno de Bruno, tall, straight and idiotically handsome. She began to laugh. She laughed and slowly shook her head from side to side. After all the things she'd been through – fighting cut-throat robbers, wading through marshes, bonking guards and everything else she'd done to marry Bruno – she suddenly realized he was a fool.

Princess Saramanda frowned for the first time in this story. 'She's gone mad!' she said. 'She's making it all up. Guards, take her away!'

Then Belinda stopped laughing, for Knackerleevee was still bound to the cart and she had unfinished business. As the guards pressed forward, Belinda slipped down from the horse and faced them. Hubert shut his eyes. He was beginning to feel rather sorry for the palace guards. He couldn't bear to watch, but he heard the thuds and groans and moans. He heard the screech of armour as it clanged against the walls of the hall. He heard the yells and screams as one by one and two by two the guards were put out of action.

Meanwhile Knackerleevee sat in the cart and grunted with satisfaction, a broad grin on his hairy face. King Krust, Saramanda and Bruno did a slow retreat up the staircase, and by the time Belinda had laid out the last guard they were on the balcony. Belinda climbed into the cart and untied her Bogle companion. Knackerleevee stretched his arms and legs and rubbed his chest.

'You said you'd teach me,' he reminded Belinda.

'I will, I will. Now, come with me. We have one more thing to do.' She got down from the cart and ran lightly up the stairs.

'Don't run away, brave king!' she cried after the disappearing royals. 'I know it wasn't your fault, and I mean you no harm.'

The king stopped and came creeping sheepishly back. 'I think you can see now that it was I who defeated the Bogle.'

King Krust nodded anxiously. 'And so I claim my prize,' said Belinda evenly. 'Marriage to Prince Bruno de Bruno and half the kingdom.'

At this the prince stepped forward as if to protest, but Knackerleevee rushed forward, seized the prince by the collar and dangled him over the balcony. 'Don't say a word,' hissed the Bogle, 'or you'll wish you knew how to fly!' Bruno's open mouth shut with a loud snap.

Saramanda looked as white as a ghost. Just when she thought she'd succeeded too. King Krust turned to her and shrugged. 'What can I do?' he murmured.

Belinda gave a little smile. 'I'll tell you what you can do. I have passed the test and so I win Bruno and half the kingdom. Fine. I now wish to give Bruno away. I don't think he'll be at all suitable. Saramanda can have him and I hope they'll be very happy.' Knackerleevee's eyes boggled in disbelief. 'As for half the kingdom,' said Belinda evenly. 'I'll have the half with the diamond mine, thank you very much.' King Krust almost had a heart attack at this, so Belinda turned to the marble balcony and raised her arm.

'Haaa-AKK!' there was a splinter of breaking stone and half the balcony plummeted down to the hall floor and shattered.

'Yes, yes, yes!' cried the king. 'The half with the diamond mine! That's fine – lovely! Oh, how wonderful! What a dear, sweet, kind, beautiful, beautiful princess you are,' he cried, now down on his knees and kissing Belinda's hand rapturously.

Belinda grinned down at Hubert. 'Come on then, you two,' she cried cheerfully. 'Let's be off to our new kingdom. I need a good bodyguard. In fact, you can be my army, Knackerleevee. And Hubert can come and paint pictures of my new kingdom for me. And I shall send for Hiro Ono to teach you karate, Knackerleevee. My parents may even come to tea – you never know!'

They went down to the old cart, hitched up the horse, climbed on board and trundled out of the palace, leaving King Krust still on his knees, Saramanda and Bruno staring at each other with stupefied grins on their faces and thirty-eight guards lying unconscious on the floor with large dents all over their armour.

The karate princess had made her mark.

'Uncle, it's almost midnight,' Belinda pointed out.

'Quite so. I must say it's been an excellent day, has it not?'

'It certainly has,' said Hubert. 'We've had a fantastic adventure, not without its hairy bits I might add . . .'

'Oh! You mean the Bogle,' Uncle Dudless said seriously, and everyone burst out laughing.

'What? What did I say? Something funny? Did I make a joke? What was it? Oh, I am a one!'

It was while they were all falling about with laughter that the Duchess of Dork appeared at the top of the grand staircase. She gazed down at the noisy throng below her, as if she'd just found a mouse in her soup.

'I say!' cried the Duchess, plucking the cheese from her ears. 'People have been coming and going for days, and now there's dancing in the hall. What on earth has been going on? Will someone please tell me?'

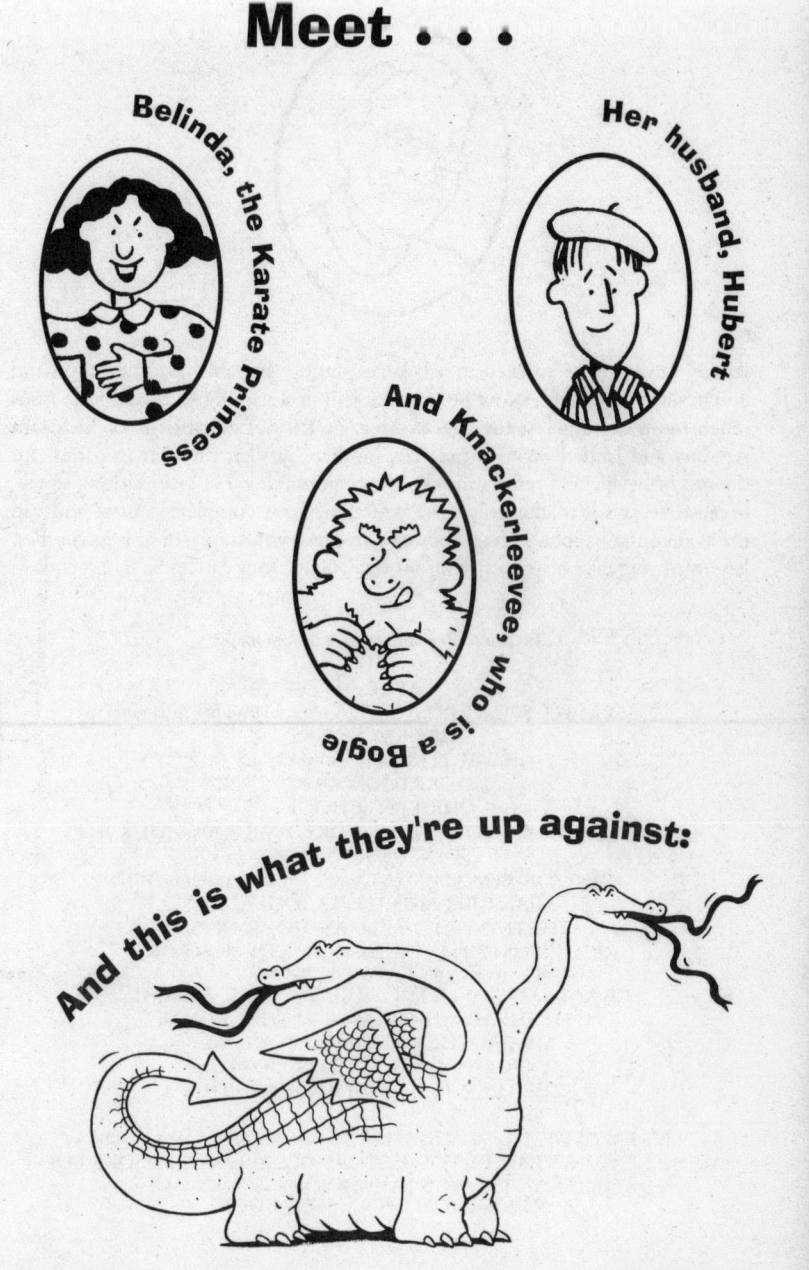

Jeremy Strong once worked in a bakery, putting the jam into three thousand doughnuts every night. Now he puts the jam in stories instead, which he finds much more exciting. At the age of three, he fell out of a first-floor bedroom window and landed on his head. His mother says that this damaged him for the rest of his life and refuses to take any responsibility. He loves writing stories because he says it is 'the only time you alone have complete control and can make anything happen'. His ambition is to make you laugh (or at least snuffle). Jeremy Strong lives near Bath with his wife, Gillie, four cats and a flying cow.

Are you feeling silly enough to read more?

BATPANTS!
THE BATTLE FOR CHRISTMAS (A Cosmic Pyjamas Adventure)
THE BEAK SPEAKS
BEWARE! KILLER TOMATOES
CARTOON KID
CHICKEN SCHOOL
CHRISTMAS CHAOS FOR THE HUNDRED-MILE-AN-HOUR DOG
DINOSAUR POX
DOCTOR BONKERS! (A Cosmic Pyjamas Adventure)
GIANT JIM AND THE HURRICANE
THE HUNDRED-MILE-AN-HOUR DOG
KRANKENSTEIN'S CRAZY HOUSE OF HORROR
(A Cosmic Pyjamas Adventure)
KRAZY COW SAVES THE WORLD – WELL, ALMOST
LOST! THE HUNDRED-MILE-AN-HOUR DOG
MY BROTHER'S FAMOUS BOTTOM
MY BROTHER'S HOT CROSS BOTTOM
THERE'S A PHARAOH IN OUR BATH!

JEREMY STRONG'S LAUGH-YOUR-SOCKS-OFF JOKE BOOK
JEREMY STRONG'S LAUGH-YOUR-SOCKS-OFF EVEN MORE JOKE BOOK
JEREMY STRONG'S LAUGH-YOUR-SOCKS-OFF
CLASSROOM CHAOS JOKE BOOK

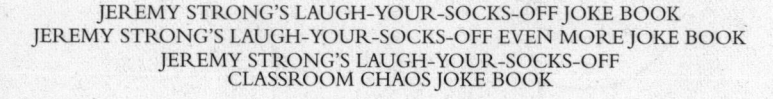

LAUGH YOUR SOCKS OFF WITH

Jeremy STRONG

The Karate Princess in MoNsta Trouble

Illustrated by Rowan Clifford

PUFFIN

PUFFIN BOOKS

Published by the Penguin Group
Penguin Books Ltd, 80 Strand, London WC2R ORL, England
Penguin Group (USA) Inc., 375 Hudson Street, New York, New York 10014, USA
Penguin Group (Canada), 90 Eglinton Avenue East, Suite 700, Toronto, Ontario, Canada M4P 2Y3
(a division of Pearson Penguin Canada Inc.)
Penguin Ireland, 25 St Stephen's Green, Dublin 2, Ireland (a division of Penguin Books Ltd)
Penguin Group (Australia), 250 Camberwell Road, Camberwell, Victoria 3124, Australia
(a division of Pearson Australia Group Pty Ltd)
Penguin Books India Pvt Ltd, 11 Community Centre,
Panchsheel Park, New Delhi – 110 017, India
Penguin Group (NZ), 67 Apollo Drive, Rosedale, Auckland 0632, New Zealand
(a division of Pearson New Zealand Ltd)
Penguin Books (South Africa) (Pty) Ltd, 24 Sturdee Avenue,
Rosebank, Johannesburg 2196, South Africa

Penguin Books Ltd, Registered Offices: 80 Strand, London WC2R ORL, England

puffinbooks.com

First published by A&C Black 1999
First published in Puffin Books 2001
Published in this flip-book edition 2011
001 – 10 9 8 7 6 5 4 3 2 1

Set in Baskerville MT 14/19
Made and printed in Great Britain by Clays Ltd, St Ives plc

British Library Cataloguing in Publication Data
A CIP catalogue record for this book is available from the British Library

ISBN: 978-0-141-33616-9

www.greenpenguin.co.uk

1 A Very Interesting Letter

The sun was shining, the sky was blue, the
summer leaves were green, and the peaceful
silence of the countryside was only broken by
the sound of singing.

'. . . Ziss leetle boat, sail, sail away, wizzer
princess and high majesty . . .'

Up and down went the raspy, wheezing
voice, as sweet and tender as sandpaper. It was
a curious sound, and it came from a curious
person. He was large and powerfully built, with
long arms, long fingers and
even longer fingernails. He
had sharp, white teeth.
He had flaring nostrils
and red eyes. And
more than anything
else, he was hairy. He
had hair everywhere,
including the soles of
his feet.

Although the noise

made by this strange creature sounded like a weasel being hit on the head, in fact he was singing. He was happy. He was singing for Belinda, the Karate Princess, and her very new husband, Hubert. Hubert and Belinda were on their honeymoon, and they had taken their best friend Knackerleevee with them.

It was Knackerleevee who was singing, in his best Bogle fashion. Knackerleevee was a Bogle of course, and that's why he was so big and strong and hairy. He was also a wee bit smelly, although he didn't pong quite so much since Belinda's mum (the Queen) had given him some aftershave for Christmas.

And now all three of them were drifting down the river, gazing up at the beautiful blue sky, and the chirping birds, and the fliffy-fluffy clouds, and the itty-pretty . . .

'I'm going mad with boredom!' Belinda suddenly yelled at the sky. 'I can't take any more of this mooning about doing nothing except admiring scenery and saying what lovely weather it is. If something interesting doesn't happen soon I shall, I shall, I shall . . .

urgh!' Belinda gave a desperate grunt, leapt from her seat and threw herself overboard. There was a loud splash and she vanished.

'Woman overboard!' cried Knackerleevee. 'Her Highshipnest is drowning!' The Bogle began rowing rapidly in as many different directions as possible in a frantic search for Belinda, but all that could be seen was a trail of bubbles on the surface.

Hubert leaned anxiously over the side, peering into the water. All at once a hand shot out of the water, grabbed the side of the boat and wrenched it so fiercely that both Knackerleevee and Hubert were cast into the water themselves.

Belinda surfaced, laughing loudly, but the Bogle was struggling and making strange gurgling noises.

'Ug, ug, I can't cug ug

urgurgle gurgle SWIM!' he finally managed to spurt out, along with a mouthful of river water and two very surprised fish.

'You are hopeless,' muttered Belinda as she grasped hold of the Bogle's hairy head and held him above the water. With Hubert's help she got Knackerleevee to the shore, where he lay in a soggy heap, panting.

'I had to stop you singing somehow,' Belinda explained. 'Anyway, you used to live in The Marsh at the End of the World – the wettest place on earth – so how come you can't swim?'

'You don't swim in a marsh,' growled Knackerleevee. 'It's not deep enough. If it was deep it wouldn't be a marsh, it would be a lake.'

Belinda grinned at him cheerfully. 'I suppose that makes sense,' she admitted. 'Well, now what shall we do?' she asked, looking at her two friends for ideas.

'I'm wet,' said Hubert. 'Why don't we go back home so we can put dry clothes on?'

'I think her Royal Majesticbit will have to hang me on the washing line,' said

4

Knackerleevee gloomily. 'It will take me weeks to dry out.'

'Don't be such a pair of miseries. It's only water. In fact it was fun. It was the best fun we've had since the wedding. We've been here two days – TWO DAYS – and done absolutely nothing. I need action. There must be something to do.'

'We could get dry,' chorused Hubert and the Bogle. 'That would be something to do.'

Belinda looked at them both and sighed. They were wet all over and limp round the

edges. She had to admit they did look just a little bit bedraggled. 'All right, we'll go home. Honestly, you two must be the wettest wets in the whole kingdom.'

'Thank you, Your Majesty,' said Hubert, a trifle coldly.

'Come on, I'll race you both!' Belinda cried and shot off across the grass towards her father's castle.

'Not running as well,' moaned Knackerleevee, watching the fast vanishing princess. 'I hate running with wet fur. It slaps around too much. Honestly, first I almost drown and now I have to slap myself with my own fur.'

'She's bored,' Hubert explained. 'She needs an adventure. I do hope she manages to find something to do soon.'

'Me too, as long as it isn't too far away, or too dangerous, or involves drowning and running. Come on, we'd better try and catch her up.'

By the time Hubert and Knackerleevee reached King Stormbelly's castle, Belinda was

already trying to use up her surplus energy.
She was pacing up and down the veranda,
beheading various ancient members of the
royal family as she went. Fortunately this was
not quite as dreadful as it sounds – they
weren't real members of the family – they were
statues that were placed all along the veranda.
However, the princess's father, King
Stormbelly, found it a trifle annoying.

'I do wish you wouldn't use your karate
around the castle,' he grumbled. 'You do
realize that you've just
chopped off your Great
Uncle Albert's head? And
there goes Auntie
Rosie! Can't you
find anything
better to do?'

'You should try
knitting, dear,' said
the Queen equably.
'Maybe you could make Knackerleevee a
cardigan.'

'A cardigan?!' Belinda burst out laughing.

'Or a pair of socks,' added the Queen, ignoring her daughter's loud snorts.

'You can't ask a great big hairy Bogle to wear a cardigan and socks!'

At this moment Knackerleevee appeared on the veranda. He stared sheepishly at the floor and twiddled his long fingernails.

'Actually, Your Worshipness, I would rather like a cardigan, I think . . . and socks. I've never had a cardigan or socks before.' The Bogle raised his sad eyes and gazed wistfully at the Queen.

'Oh, Knackerleevee – I didn't realize! I mean, I never thought – I shall knit you a cardigan at once. Come over here so I can measure your arms, and tell me what colour you'd like.' The Bogle immediately perked up and hurried over to the Queen, while Belinda threw herself into a deckchair and watched them moodily.

'I cannot believe that a great big hairy Bogle could get excited about a-a-a cardigan,' she snapped. 'And socks!' She spat out the words as if they were highly poisonous.

Hubert smiled. 'He's spent most of his life in a rather wet, rather gloomy, rather miserable marsh. A cardigan must seem quite splendid to him.'

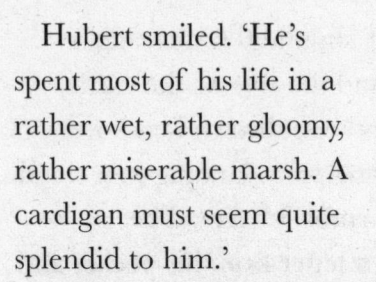

Belinda turned and looked up at her husband. Her eyes filled with tenderness. 'That's why I married you. Oh, Hubert, I know I can be horrible at times. I only think of myself and adventures. You're quite right of course. Cardigans and socks must seem very exciting to someone who's lived in a soggy marsh. It's just that . . .' her voice trailed away. 'I wish there was something really exciting to do.'

Hubert squeezed her hand. 'It would be good. You could have an adventure, and I could paint it.'

At this moment there was a loud clatter from

beyond and a lot of shouting. A messenger came galloping round the side of the castle, skidded to a halt and was thrown head-over-heels from his panting pony, landing in a cloud of dust at King Stormbelly's feet. The messenger plucked a letter from his pocket and waved it at the King.

'Urgent message from my master, the Duke,' he cried.

'Oh! A letter. How fascinating.' The King pushed a podgy finger under the seal and unrolled the battered scroll. 'Ah! It's from my brother!'

'Which brother is that, dear?' enquired the Queen, knowing that the King had seven brothers dotted about here and there.

'It's Dudless, Duke of Dork,' began Stormbelly, straining his eyes to read the childlike scrawl. The Queen was surprised.

'Really? I didn't think

Dudless could read, let alone write.'

'It is an odd letter,' admitted King Stormbelly. He showed it to Belinda. 'There – what do you make of it?'

Belinda studied the message carefully.

A slow smile spread across Belinda's face. 'At last,' she sighed dreamily. 'An adventure – something to do. Hurrah.'

Dear BroTha,
Pleze help. wee aRRbeen
~~Tokkaw Terry IT foRyd~~ TeRRoRyzed
by A MoNsta. It haz got 1 TaLe,
2 Hedz, 4 TuNgz, 2 WiNgz and 4
leggz. It goez RAAArgh! aNd Maks
us RuN away (verryfast) Becoz if It
catCHes aNyWuN iT EETs tHeml It
haz Eaten My ARmee and my PeT
raBBit Tony. We doNt lik iT verry
MUCH. But we're scaReDy kats so
PlEse HELPp. SeNd yor verry bestest
MAN.
P.S. THeRe is a prise foR tHe persuN
who ~~spiffle~~ spifflykates tHe MoNsta
LuV and kiSSez
Dudless, Duck of Dork

2 Introducing Dudless, Duke of Dork

'Come on!' cried the Karate Princess. 'There's a two-headed MoNsta on the loose, eating armies and pet rabbits. And there's a prize too – so hurry up!'

'But what about my cardigan?' Knackerleevee was crestfallen.

The Queen patted Knackerleevee on one hairy arm. 'It's all right, dear, you run along. I've got all the measurements I need. By the time you get back I might even have finished it.'

'Now look here,' steamed King Stormbelly, 'you're on your honeymoon. You're supposed to be relaxing.'

'If I relax any more my head will fall off.'

'I do wish you were more like your other sisters. I mean to say, they're all . . .'

'Beautiful?' suggested Belinda.

'Exactly. And they're . . .'

'Witty?' Belinda put in.

'Quite so. And they're . . .'

'Boring?' said Belinda slyly.

'Definitely! Heh – no! I mean definitely not! You-you,' stuttered the King, 'you were trying to trick me then, weren't you?'

Belinda gave her father an innocent glance. The Queen laughed quietly. 'I think you must admit dear that your youngest daughter is every bit as clever as her sisters – if not cleverer.'

'Doh! Codswallop and poppywhatsits. If you want to go dancing off to get chewed up by a two-headed MoNsta then don't expect me to stop you.'

'But you are trying to stop me,' Belinda pointed out.

'Ah! Ah!' cried the King, wagging a finger at his daughter. 'I was, but I'm not any longer, and I hope he eats you up in one mouthful. See if I care!'

'Thank you, Daddy.' Belinda smiled, kissing her father on his bald head and making him blush furiously. 'I shall take that as your blessing on our dangerous mission. Come on, Hubert. You'd better go and pack all your paint things.'

So it was that a short time later the three adventurers climbed on to their horses (Knackerleevee's horse was an extra large, extra strong beast called Goliath), and set off to find Stormbelly's brother and the dreadful MoNsta.

Hubert was carrying a big, sharp sword. Knackerleevee was also armed to the teeth. (Actually he was armed *with* his teeth – and his long talons and great strength.) But the only weapon that Belinda had was her bare hands.

Belinda was not known as the Karate Princess for nothing. She had been taught karate by Hiro Ono, the most famous karate expert in this book – even in the whole world, and she had been his best pupil. In fact, so good was Belinda at karate that she had defeated (in the past, and not all at the same

14

time) the merciless Cut-Throat Robbers, a fearful steam-dragon, and a whole army of sumo-wrestlers, not to mention the odious Grand Oompah of Pomposity.

Of course being good at karate was not always quite enough to get by on, but luckily Belinda was also cunning, and she had her two very good companions, Hubert and Knackerleevee, to help her. Now, as they approached her uncle's castle, she had high hopes for an excellent adventure.

The Duke of Dork looked much like his brother Stormbelly, except that he was shorter, fatter, balder and had a very high squeaky voice. This made him seem even more stupid than he really was, and in reality the Duke of Dork was very stupid indeed. He was so useless that Belinda felt quite sorry for him. 'Dorinda!' cried the Duke. 'It's you!'

'BELINDA,' corrected the Karate Princess. 'You always call me Dorinda, and my name is Belinda.'

'Sorry, so sorry. What a wonderful funeral that was! I did enjoy myself. Lovely dress!' The

Duke gave Knackerleevee a sly prod. 'This must be your new wife? Charming, but a bit too hairy for my taste, and far too tall. Guard! Fetch me a ladder so that I can kiss the bride.' Knackerleevee shot an alarmed look at the princess.

'It was my WEDDING, Uncle, not a funeral. And please meet Hubert, my HUSBAND, who is not at all hairy.'

'Oh silly me, of course. Well, my dears, it is lovely to see you. Are you on your jammy?'

The three friends glanced at each other. What was a jammy? The Duke observed their

puzzlement. 'Oh you must know what I mean,' he said airily. 'Maybe I've got the word wrong. I know it's something to do with jam, or is it marmalade? Honey, maybe?'

'Perhaps you mean "honeymoon", ' suggested Hubert politely.

'Of course, yes, that's the one. Is that why you're here? Are you going to spend some of your honeyspoon with us? Splendid!' The Duke of Dork beamed at the Duchess, who Belinda suddenly realized was sitting very quietly in a corner, playing cards with herself.

Belinda hadn't noticed her at all. She hadn't taken part in any of the conversation so far, which Belinda thought was a little strange. Then she remembered that the Duchess always put large chunks of cheese in her ear, as ear plugs, so that she didn't have to listen to her husband's constant nonsense.

'Actually,' said Belinda, 'we've come on another matter.'

'Oh yes? Is it teatime? Have you come for tea?'

'No, Uncle. We haven't come for tea. It's something altogether more dangerous.'

'Ah!' The Duke's eyes lit up. 'Of course! You mean supper. You've come for supper!'

Hubert leaned forward, looking puzzled. 'Is supper dangerous around these parts?' he asked. The Duke nodded seriously.

'Indeed it is. I keep poking myself in the eye with my fork. Daft thing, if you ask me. I'd rather use my fingers.'

'Why don't you?' suggested Hubert. The Duke of Dork took a step back, gazed at Hubert with utter astonishment, stepped forward again, flung his short arms round the painter and hugged him.

'Of course! Why didn't I think of that? Excellent

idea! Oho, I can't wait for supper now, especially if you're coming too.'

'We haven't come for supper,' Belinda explained patiently. 'Don't you remember, Uncle? You wrote to my father about a problem you have here – a big problem.'

'The downstairs toilet doesn't flush any more?'

'No, it wasn't the toilet.'

'It's that mouse in the kitchen, isn't it – the one that keeps eating the Duchess's best Camembert?'

'No, it's not the mouse in the kitchen.'

'Oh.' The Duke gave her a grumpy glance. 'Well, I don't know then. Give me a clue.'

Knackerleevee sighed impatiently.

'It's got two heads and goes "Raaaargh!" ' he growled.

'It's the cat!' cried the Duke with a huge smile.

'NO!' yelled Belinda, finally losing all patience. 'It's the two-headed MoNsta that's eaten your army and your rabbit.'

The Duke of Dork turned very pale and

began to tremble, and since he was mostly made of fat he trembled quite spectacularly. His three chins wobbled, his cheeks quivered, his bottom bounced about and his belly shook like an enormous jelly.

'Ssssssh! It might hear you.'

'Is it near by?' whispered Knackerleevee. The Duke shook his head. 'Then why do we have to be quiet?' The Duke thought about this, his forehead frowning more and more with each passing second. At last he shook his head.

'I don't know,' he admitted. 'Could you ask me again tomorrow, when I've had time to think about it? I'm afraid I'm rather confused. I don't understand this at all,' he complained. 'Why are you here?'

'We've come to rid you of the MoNsta,' Belinda said simply. 'You sent a note to Daddy asking for help. Well, I'm the help.'

'You?'

'Yes, me and my two friends here, Hubert and Knackerleevee.'

'But, but, you're a princess,' stuttered the Duke.

'Yes.'

'Princesses don't fight MoNstas.'

'Why not?'

'Er, it's um, it's . . .' The poor Duke shook his head again. For several seconds he looked totally stunned, and then a bright thought occurred to him. 'Look here, you can't fight the MoNsta because you can't have the prize.'

'And why can't I have the prize?' asked Belinda.

'Well, it would be so silly, wouldn't it?'

'Why? What is the prize?'

'It's my daughter. Whoever defeats the MoNsta can marry my daughter, Taloola. You can't marry my daughter now, can you?' The Duke beamed at Belinda triumphantly. 'Of course you can't. You're already married!'

The Bogle let out an enormous groan. He was beginning to think it would be a great

relief to everyone if the MoNsta did eat the
Duke. Belinda gave Hubert a look of despair.
She was about to start arguing with the Duke
when a door at the far end of the royal
chamber burst open and in came Taloola.

At least, she didn't exactly *come* in. It was
more like a small explosion of golden hair and
red lipstick and mouth and noise and flailing
body. Not only was Taloola glamorous, but she
was tubby – in fact 'tubular' would probably be

a better description. (It was something she had inherited from her father.)

'Popsicle!' cried Taloola, with tears streaming down her face and making rather a mess of her eyeliner and cheek-blush. 'I can't stand any more of this. Everywhere I go there are princes trying to marry me. The castle is full of them! They're even sleeping in cupboards now! I will not marry a handsome prince, not even if the two-headed MoNsta eats everyone in the country; not even if you put sardines in my chocolate mousse; not in a million, zillion years. You know I love Gordon the goatherd, and I shall never marry anyone but him!'

With this magnificent outburst Taloola threw herself howling at her father's feet.

3 Enter the Handsome Prince

It was Hubert who went to Taloola's rescue. He leaned over her, crooning gently.

'There, there, it's all right, Taloola ... don't cry.' Then He made an almost fatal mistake – he tried to lift Taloola to her feet. He managed to raise her top half from the floor, but couldn't manage her legs. He then succeeded in lifting both her legs, but couldn't manage her top half. After a couple of failed attempts he gave Knackerleevee a desperate look. The Bogle strode over, flung one arm round Taloola's waist and swept her from the floor.

'Oh!' simpered Taloola, fluttering her false eyelashes at the Bogle. 'You are strong! But

why are you wearing a fur coat? It's the middle of summer. And what's that funny smell?'

'It's not a fur coat. Knackerleevee is a Bogle, and that's his real skin,' Belinda explained.

Taloola gave a startled shriek and hurriedly pulled a pair of glasses from her little handbag. She took one look, slapped the Bogle's face, cried, 'Unhand me, you villainous beast!' and fainted. The Bogle dumped her on the ground and folded his hairy arms.

'I'm not picking her up again,' he growled.

The Duke clapped his hands and four guards appeared. They heaved the unfortunate girl into a seat, where she sat slumped over to one side. Belinda decided that now would be a good opportunity to ask her uncle why the castle was stuffed with princes.

'It's very simple,' explained the Duke. 'The first prince to kill the MoNsta will marry my daughter. You wouldn't believe how many princes have turned up. The castle is crawling with them.'

'And have the princes seen Taloola?' Belinda couldn't help asking.

'Of course,' said the Duke. 'They love her, adore her, worship her. Of course there is the added attraction of one million gold coins – but I'm sure it is Taloola that the princes are really after.'

'Of course,' murmured Belinda. 'But what about Gordon the goatherd?'

'Don't be ridiculous. A duke's daughter can't marry a goatherd.'

'Why not?'

'Why not? I'll tell you why not. Because er, er . . . they smell! That's why not.'

'Everybody smells,' Belinda pointed out.

'Ah yes, but um, er . . . they've got horns!' cried Dudless. Belinda shook her head.

'No, Uncle: a goat has horns, not a goatherd.'

'Well it's just not done. Ladies in our family always marry princes,' he blustered.

'I didn't. I married an artist.'

'Splrrrrrrrrgh!' The Duke of Dork almost choked. 'My daughter will marry a prince,' he shouted. Then his face crumpled. 'I can't wait for her to leave home. She's so –

overwhelming, so moody and mountainous. I can't cope any more, and her mother never listens to anything except cheese. Then this dreadful MoNsta appeared – it really is terrible you know – and we all thought we were going to die. In fact I did die, but then my butler woke me up with a cup of tea and said I'd been asleep. And then I got this idea and it really is rather clever you see, because all these princes have arrived here, and they've got to kill the MoNsta and marry Taloola, and then they'll take her away and everything will be peaceful once more.'

Belinda and Hubert and the Bogle were by this time sitting at the Duke's feet, listening

intently to his tale of woe.

'Why can't Gordon the goatherd fight the MoNsta and then marry Taloola?' asked Hubert.

'Oh I don't think that would work at all,' said Dudless. 'Have you met Gordon? He's a vegetarian. Built like a stick insect. He couldn't hurt a fly.'

'Then why not let us deal with the MoNsta?' suggested Belinda. 'And if we get rid of this dreadful MoNsta then Taloola can marry Gordon and everyone will be happy.'

The Duke of Dork brightened visibly for a moment. Then his face fell. 'What about all the princes that have already arrived. I can't just send them away.'

'Don't worry,' said Hubert. 'Belinda and Knackerleevee will deal with the MoNsta long before the princes get anywhere near it. Then Taloola can marry Gordon and leave home, and everyone will be happy ever after. How's that?'

Dudless remained cheerful this time, and the three friends could see that their little

adventure was going to be fairly straightforward after all. Unfortunately though, they had rather underestimated the skill and determination of a certain Prinz Blippenbang.

Prinz Blippenbang was a typical handsome prince. He was stunningly strong and good-looking. He had blue eyes, blond hair, a firm, jutting jaw, a straight back and broad shoulders.

He had a powerful chest that rippled with muscles, and even more rippling muscles down each arm and leg.

All these things made him sound too good to be true, and of course he was too good to be true. In fact, he wasn't good at all. He was bad through and through. Here are just a few of the things that Prinz Blippenbang had done in the past.

He had stolen his grandmother's ear-trumpet, filled it with rice pudding and given it back. She almost died of shock when she found

rice pudding pouring out of her ear – she thought her brain was falling out of her head.

He had almost drowned his little sister's tortoise in the palace pond by making a submarine out of cardboard and using the tortoise as a test pilot. The submarine sank at once and the tortoise only managed to escape by kicking the sides to bits.

He had frittered away most of his father's fortune by placing bets on such strange things as: 'A fairy-godmother will arrive on Tuesday morning and turn all your pyjamas into gold' or, 'It will rain every day for two hundred years, starting tomorrow.' He could never resist a bet, no matter how ridiculous.

Now Prinz Blippenbang had run out of money altogether, and he was desperate to get his hands on Taloola's fortune, but not on Taloola herself. The Prinz was shrewd and clever. He knew that there would be other princes after the money and, more importantly, he knew that the MoNsta was not going to be an easy victim. MoNstas that eat armies and pet rabbits are not the sort of MoNstas to go

all weak at the knees and start begging for
mercy if you simply point a sword at them.
No, this MoNsta was going to be
TROUBLESOME.

And that was why Prinz Blippenbang had
brought a bazooka with him.

A bazooka is like a small, portable
cannon. It is a very powerful
weapon. When the
bazooka is loaded and
the trigger is pulled
something nasty happens. A
cannonball comes whizzing
out at top speed and flies
towards its target in a very
dangerous manner. When
it hits the target the result is something that
looks like a mixture of scrambled egg, tomato
sauce and lots of smoke.

Any MoNsta facing a bazooka like the one
Prinz Blippenbang had, was going to be in
dead trouble. In other words, in trouble and
dead. The MoNsta was as good as this already,
and he knew it.

When Prinz Blippenbang and all the other princes realized that a girl was going to challenge the MoNsta they almost laughed their socks off. 'But you're a girly!' they cried. 'You can't find the MoNsta!' This was rather stupid of them, but Belinda kept her cool.

'Do you believe in unidentified flying objects?' she asked.

'Of course not,' they scoffed. 'Don't be so silly.'

'I can prove they exist,' said Belinda, smiling. Knowing what was about to happen, Hubert and

Knackerleevee both looked for a safe place to shelter. 'I'll show you,' she said. She waded in amongst the crowd of princes and soon royalties and highnesses were flying right, left and centre. Some flapped their arms like birds, and some whirled round like helicopters, and several made very loud jet noises as they flew through the air.

'Neeeyyaaaaargh!'

The only thing they had in common was that they all crashed with loud thuds and bangs and then limped away moaning and groaning, looking for bandages and sympathy.

Prinz Blippenbang watched with cunning interest as the Karate Princess coolly despatched seventeen princes. Here was someone who might well interfere with his plans. He was going to have to keep a close eye on Belinda and her companions. If he wanted to claim the MoNsta for himself and win those million gold coins, then he would have to do something about the Karate Princess and her friends – like get rid of them.

Prinz Blippenbang patted his bazooka. He was looking forward to putting it into action.

4 The MoNsta Makes a Visit

As Belinda dusted herself down she watched the last of the brave princes crawl away with a pained whimper.

'Can we look yet?' asked Hubert. 'Is it safe?'

'Of course,' laughed Belinda. Knackerleevee banged his hands together.

'You are a warrior, Princessness,' he bellowed cheerfully, but Hubert was more wary.

'I do wish you wouldn't do that. You might at least warn them in advance.'

'What good would that do? They'd just go on laughing and poking fun at me. I hate being made fun of.'

'I'll bear it in mind,' murmured Hubert. 'But maybe you should wear a sign on your jacket – something like: DANGEROUS – DO NOT APPROACH. Anyway, let's get on with the matter in hand. What are we going to do about the MoNsta?'

'We're going to kill it,' declared the Bogle,

making it sound a lot easier than it was going to be.

'How? We're talking about a creature that can fly. It's got two heads and four tongues, which apparently are half a mile long and very sticky. They flick out and things stick to them and then the MoNsta eats them. Big MoNstas with sticky tongues aren't nice, Knackerleevee. I've heard that it's as big as a house.'

'That doesn't mean anything,' the Bogle grumbled. 'What kind of house? It could be a house for a mouse, a mouse-house . . .'

'Don't be silly. Mice don't have hice, I mean houses,' said Hubert. 'You know perfectly well I mean a big house, a proper house.'

Belinda listened to this argument with increasing frustration.

'This isn't getting us anywhere. We need a plan.' But before they could put their heads together loud cries began to ring throughout the castle.

The MoNsta was on the move. It had been seen, hovering over the distant hills and heading towards the castle. Dudless was having

a panic attack. It was easy to tell that he was in
a state of high anxiety because he was standing
on top of the dining table with a paper bag

over his head so that he couldn't see. He was
trembling all over, so much so that even the
table was quaking. He held a bucket in one
hand and he was fiercely brandishing a mop
with the other.

'Stand back or I'll shoot!' he yelled. 'You
can't get me, you horrible MoNsta!'

'Uncle!' cried Belinda, hurrying into the
room. 'It's all right. The MoNsta is still miles

away.' The trembling stopped and the mop was lowered.

'Are you sure?' asked the Duke.

'Quite sure. Anyway, you are surrounded by brave princes who have all come here to protect you. Even now some of them are riding out to meet the MoNsta and fight it.'

'Oh? That's a relief.' Dudless pulled the bag off his head. 'Mind you, it won't do any good, Dorinda.'

'BELINDA,' chorused the three friends.

'It will slurp them all up, just like it slurped up my army. It's horrible. Its tongues are all yellow and purple, you know, and slimy.' Hubert helped the Duke down from the table.

'Do you know where it lives?' he asked.

'Afraid not. Nobody knows. Everyone is too scared to follow it. Besides, it flies away. We think it goes off somewhere to sleep after it's eaten, like a snake.'

The Karate Princess frowned. 'This is going to be more difficult than I thought. I was hoping we might be able to catch the beast in its lair, while it's asleep, but if nobody knows

where it lives that will be difficult.'

'We can follow it, Highship.'

'We can't fly,' Hubert pointed out.

'I could throw you,' suggested Knackerleevee darkly. He was getting a bit tired of Hubert always being cleverer than he was. He knew he wasn't terribly clever, but he didn't like other people to think so.

Belinda wasn't even listening to them. She had ideas of her own. 'What we need is some string.'

'String? What are you going to do? Tie the MoNsta up?' cried Dudless. 'You can't tie up a MoNsta with little bits of string.' Belinda ignored him.

'I want every bit of string there is in the castle,' she said.

'I think you're very silly,' Dudless replied, stubbornly folding his arms.

Belinda's face darkened. She glanced briefly round the room and her eyes fell upon a big oak armoury cupboard standing at the far end. She approached it slowly, softly and silently. As she drew nearer her whole body became a

focus of energy, her muscles tightly sprung. She stopped for a moment, her body coiling itself up, and then she launched her attack. With a few bounds she had thrown herself at the cupboard.

'Haa-akkkk!' Her legs snapped out in front of her and both feet thundered against the cupboard with such force that the doors split apart and the contents spilled out with a noise like a thousand crashing saucepans.

Twelve suits of armour crashed to the floor, followed by helmets and swords and spears and bows and arrows. Finally the cupboard itself teetered forward and crashed to the ground on top of the armour. The Karate Princess turned back to her uncle, eyes blazing.

'I want every bit of

string in the castle,' she repeated. 'Now.'

'No problem,' squeaked the Duke, hurrying off to give the order. 'At once. Your wish is my command.'

'I know I'm not very bright,' muttered the Bogle, 'but why do we need lots of string?'

Belinda sat on the edge of the table. 'It doesn't matter if you are clever or not, Knackerleevee. You are very strong, and a true and trusted friend, and that is more important than being clever.' The Bogle gave Hubert a delighted smirk while Belinda went on.

'I reckon our best hope of defeating the MoNsta is to catch it in its lair, while it's sleeping off one of its heavy meals – do you agree?' The others nodded. 'Our problem is to track the beast down after it has flown away. This may not be a very good idea, and it may not work, but I can't think of anything else at the moment and the pair of you are too busy sniping at each other to be much use. We tie the string together to make one very, very big ball of string and we tie one end of the string to the MoNsta's tail. The MoNsta flies away.

The string unwinds. We hold on to the other end of the string and when the MoNsta goes to sleep we follow the string until we find it.'

Once again the Bogle went into raptures of delight, even kissing Belinda on the forehead. 'You are so clever, Highboat!' Hubert sighed and gave his wife a pale smile.

'Suppose we run out of string while the MoNsta is still flying?'

'Suppose we don't?'

'And how do we tie string on to the tail of a horrible man-eating MoNsta without it knowing?'

Belinda jumped down from the table.

'Don't be so negative, Hubert. I've already said it might not work. Look, I'll do the string-on-the-tail bit, if you're scared.'

'I'm not scared for me,' Hubert said. 'I'm scared for you. We only got married a few days ago, and here you are putting your life in danger.'

The princess's face softened and she hugged Hubert closely, while Knackerleevee turned rather red,

gave the pair a soppy grin and sighed.

'Aaaaah. That's so sweet.'

But this touching scene was rudely
interrupted by an ear-piercing scream. 'The
MoNsta is here! It's outside the castle walls!
Pull up the drawbridge! Pull the curtains! Hide
under your beds!'

The three companions rushed over to the
window, and there was the MoNsta in full view.
They stared in
silent awe, until at
last Hubert spoke.

'That is a big MoNsta,' he whispered fearfully.

It was like a brontosaurus, but its skin was scaly, like a crocodile. Its legs were very short and stout, so that its belly trailed upon the ground, crushing anything beneath. Two large wings sprouted from its back. They were folded against its sides, but as the beast darted forward its wings spread and cracked the air with stiff blows.

Behind the MoNsta its tail stretched out, long and scaly, whipping angrily from side to side. And most fearsome of all were its two heads and four tongues.

Each head was on the end of a long neck, and was shaped like that of a giant snake. Cold, unblinking eyes glistened fiercely as it scanned the countryside for food – a cow here, a sheep there, a brave prince or two, complete with horse – all were suddenly engulfed by one of the four flickering tongues. Hubert had been told that each tongue was half a mile long – this was a bit of an exaggeration, although they certainly gave that impression, and if you happened to be the person stuck to

the tongue, you probably wouldn't care if it was half a mile long or only a few centimetres.

'That is nasty,' muttered Knackerleevee. Belinda's heart sank. For the first time in her life she felt utterly defeated. This was a MoNsta from hell.

The Duke of Dork came striding back into the room, followed by several servants clutching masses of string. 'I've brought your string Dorinda,' he announced cheerfully. 'I say, what are you all staring at?'

The others made way for Dudless as he came to the window. He peered out, took one look at the MoNsta and slid to the floor.

'I know just how he feels,' murmured Belinda. She could almost hear her own heart screaming at her – 'Let me out! I want to go home!' But she told herself to be strong and began work on the string. 'Come on. Let's get this lot tied together. There's no time to lose.'

From a dark doorway Prinz Blippenbang's eyes narrowed. This was going so well! That silly little girl

could do all the work and lead him to the MoNsta, then he could take over with his trusty bazooka.

5 How to Play 'Pin the Tail on the MoNsta'

In the castle courtyard an astonishing scene was taking place. At least forty princes (and for some reason many of them were wearing large plasters or bandages) were pulling on their shining armour. On went the breastplates. On went the metal shoes and leggings, and finally the heavy helmets.

They climbed on to their horses, who were themselves decked out in armour and coloured robes. The princely knights grabbed their lances and spears and swords and shields and generally armed themselves to the hilt with as many weapons as they could carry. They were ready to do battle.

'Lower the drawbridge!' they cried.

Chains banged and rattled through stone channels and with a creak and a groan the great iron drawbridge came clanking down across the moat. A moment later it echoed to the sound of horses' hooves as the valiant

princes rode out to do battle with the MoNsta.
Behind them all came Belinda and Hubert and
the Bogle, carrying no weapons at all except a
very large ball of string.

And behind them came Prinz Blippenbang,
clutching his trusty bazooka.

The brave princes formed a miniature army,
and they went charging towards the MoNsta,
lances at the tilt. Meanwhile, the three
companions, still being shadowed by the Prinz,
made a wide detour, in a bid to get beyond and

behind the fearsome creature.

The princes did not seem to have much of a strategy for attacking the MoNsta. They would rush at it headlong, but as soon as a slurpy tongue came anywhere near them they would turn tail and gallop away screaming. Belinda watched all this from a comfortable distance.

'It's like watching two-year-olds on the beach running away from the waves,' she observed. Nevertheless she was worried. 'I do wish that horrible beast would keep its tail still.'

'You'll have to come with me,' she told the Bogle. 'You might just be strong enough to hold down the end of its tail long enough for me to tie on one end of the string.'

'Not even Knackerleevee is that strong,' Hubert pointed out.

'Don't argue with me, Hubert,' snapped Belinda. 'I need somebody's help out there.

Apart from anything else, someone is going to have to put their finger on the knot so that I can tie it tightly.'

'Put their finger on the knot!' Hubert almost burst out laughing, but he saw the angry look on Belinda's face and wisely kept quiet.

The Bogle grabbed the ball of string and quietly padded after the princess as she began to creep up behind the MoNsta, whose tail was thrashing and crashing about like a shark out of water. This was certainly going to be a tricky operation.

Belinda ran quickly from one hiding place to another, trying to keep an eye on both the MoNsta's heads at once. She approached from the left and then, just as she was tiptoeing up to the tail – PROYYOINNGGG! Up in the air it went and came crashing down in a cloud of dust away to her right.

Belinda approached from the right. She crept towards the MoNsta holding out the string in front of her and was almost there when – WHAANNGGG! Up went the tail again and came down with a tremendous bang

in the centre ground. Belinda approached from
the centre, but didn't even get halfway there
before the tail was off on another sky-bound
journey.

This happened over and over again, until the
Karate Princess finally lost her temper
altogether. 'Oh for goodness sake!'
she bellowed. 'Will you
PLEASE keep still!'
Both heads of the MoNsta
whipped round and four cold
eyes fixed the three friends.
Two mouths opened. Two
horrible hisses came from each
throat and out shot four tongues, like purple
and yellow whips.

'Uh-oh!' cried
Belinda, and
hastily
ran away
so fast that she
overtook both
Knackerleevee
and Hubert. They

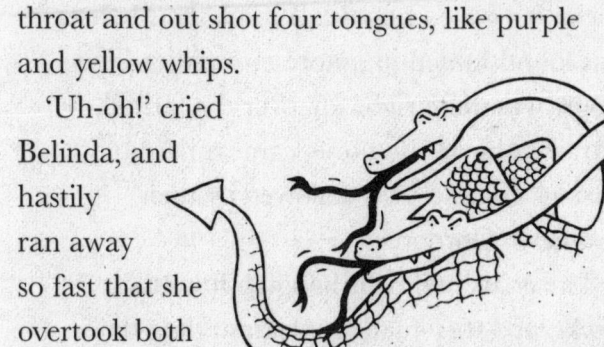

threw themselves behind a large rock and lay there panting, while the tips of four tongues writhed about the ground nearby, searching.

'Temper, temper,' muttered Hubert reproachfully.

'I know, I know.' Belinda had to agree with him. She knew her temper was her weak point. When she had been a karate student her teacher – the famous Hiro Ono – had often told her to shut her mind to her temper. 'Lose your temper and lose the battle,' he used to tell her. And just now he had almost been proved right.

Knackerleevee peered out from behind the rock. 'It's gone,' he said. 'I think the MoNsta has found something more interesting. The Bogle was quite right for, over the far hill, attracted by all the noise, came a herd of curious goats, closely followed by their goatherd, Gordon.

The goats had bells hanging from their necks, and they made a pleasant ding-dong noise as they trotted down the hillside. The MoNsta seemed very attracted to the noise too,

because it had
turned away from its search
for Belinda and her friends, and was
now gazing with immense pleasure at the
sight of dinner trotting straight towards it.

Gordon of course was going frantic. 'Come
back you daft animals. That's the MoNsta! It's
not a vegetarian like me! It will have you all for
dinner!' But his shouts were in vain. On went
the goats, bleating merrily, while the MoNsta
became intently quiet. It crouched down on its
great belly, breathing as quietly as possible. Its
four tongues lay curled up and ready, and its
tail lay as still as a dead python.

'Now's our chance,' whispered Belinda.
'Come on, Knackerleevee.' They came out
from behind their rock and began the long

53

creep forward. It seemed to take ages, but still the MoNsta had all its attention fixed firmly on Gordon's goats, who were wandering ever closer. Belinda urged herself on, she had to get the string on the tail before the MoNsta went into action, or realized what was happening at its rear.

At last Belinda was standing right by the tail-tip, and even though it was the tip it was still almost as big as Belinda herself. She grasped the end of the string and gently wound it round and round. She tied a knot. 'Quick, put your finger there,' she ordered, and Knackerleevee dutifully obliged.

Maybe the goats had just got within range, or maybe the MoNsta felt the Bogle's long, sharp nails, but suddenly the tail rose in the air, with Belinda and the Bogle still clinging to it. The MoNsta roared and hissed and the four tongues shot out.

'Blaaaah!' bleated the goats.

'Raaaargh!' hissed the MoNsta.

'Yaaaargh!' yelled Belinda and Knackerleevee.

Down came the tail with a bone-crunching bang. Knackerleevee rolled away into the bushes half-conscious, but Belinda managed to soak up most of the fall with a well-timed judo roll. She sprang to her feet and grabbed the ball of string. The MoNsta already had a mouthful of fresh goat. Poor Gordon the goatherd was in despair, but there was nothing he could do except make sure that he didn't go the same way as his goats. Even the knights in shining armour had run away back to the castle when they saw the fate of the goats. Only Prinz Blippenbang remained, peering out from a large bush. Prinz Blippenbang could feel his ultimate triumph creeping closer and closer.

With a last slurp the MoNsta smiled cheerfully and spread its great wings. They

beat the air and the huge beast slowly lifted from the ground. It rose into the air like some monstrous thunder cloud, higher and higher, with the knotted string trailing out behind, and then it flew away, accompanied by the faint sound of muffled goats' bells. Belinda unrolled the string as fast as she could. Hubert ran over and began helping.

'Are you all right?' he cried. 'I thought that was the end of you when you were whisked up in the air like that.'

'I'm OK. Just keep unwinding the string and pray that it doesn't break.'

Knackerleevee groaned and staggered to his feet.

'Urgh – I feel as if I've just been hurled to the ground by a monstrous tail.'

'Help us unwind the string!' they both shouted and he hurried over. The ball was rapidly dwindling and the MoNsta had almost vanished from view.

'We're going to run out of string!' yelled Belinda, as the last piece ran through her fingers. She grabbed the end before it could be

whisked away and she was off, half running, half jumping as she tried to keep up with the MoNsta's flight.

And then all at once the string went slack. Belinda stood on the hillside panting furiously, still clutching the string, while the others ran to catch up with her.

'You've still got it!' cried Hubert with admiration.

'Yes, but have I got it because the MoNsta has settled down to sleep, or because the string has snapped somewhere?'

'There's only one way to find out,' Hubert pointed out, but before they could set off they were suddenly confronted by a groaning Gordon, grieving for his goats.

'All my goats! Every single one! Gobbled up, like . . . like . . . goats that have been gobbled, I suppose.'

'You have a lovely way with words,' murmured Hubert.

'I'm in shock,' cried Gordon. 'My goats have been gobbled.'

'Pull yourself together,' Belinda ordered.

57

'What would Taloola say if she saw you like this?'

Gordon gave a mighty sniff.

'You're right. I must pull myself together.' He gazed with curiosity at the length of string in Belinda's hand.

'Where's the balloon?' he asked.

'There isn't a balloon on the end of this string,' Belinda explained. 'There's a MoNsta, at least we hope that is what is on the end, because we intend to follow the string to the MoNsta's lair and then we shall kill it before it can do any more damage.'

'Then I must come with you!' cried Gordon, 'so that I can see that justice is done, for the sake of my goats.'

With that they began following the string.

Not so very far behind them Prinz Blippenbang emerged from behind his rock and began discreetly to follow the MoNsta hunters.

'I'm coming too,' he muttered quietly, 'because where Belinda goes, I go, but what Belinda does I shall claim I did myself. Then I

shall have the money and Taloola. I shall keep
the money of course, but Taloola can jump off
a cliff for all I care. Hee hee hee!'

6 The Princess in the Pothole

The string led them over the first hill and on to the brow of the second hill where for the first time they were able to see a long cliff face beyond. In front of them the string stretched out through the air.

'There must be a cave or something in the cliff,' mused Hubert. He set off at a run down the hill and across a narrow gully until he reached the bottom of the cliff. 'Look, up beyond that big clump of bushes. Isn't that a hole?'

Belinda and the Bogle squinted up to where Hubert was pointing. Then they saw it – a long, dark fissure in the rock, half hidden by bushes.

'It's just about big enough for the MoNsta to crawl through,' she murmured, 'and if it's big enough for the MoNsta then it's certainly big enough for us.'

'It's much bigger inside,' Gordon

announced. Belinda looked
round, startled.

'Really? How do you
know?'

'One of my nanny
goats went in there
last year. She'd hurt
her leg and couldn't
climb down. I had
to rescue her.'
Gordon sniffed
loudly. 'Now she's back
in there again, only this
time she's gone for ever.
My poor little goats.' He
snuffled again and
hastily wiped away a
tear with his wispy
beard.

'Come on,' said Belinda.
'It's no use crying over
spilled goats' milk. Let's get up there and find
the MoNsta.' Gordon nodded bravely and they
began to climb.

61

The cliff face was crumbly, but at least there were plenty of hand and foot holds, and they were soon well on their way to the opening. Knackerleevee made the mistake of looking down to see how far they had come.

'Ohohoh,' he moaned. 'It's a long way down, Nestship. Oooh, I don't like it. My knees are going wobbly and my stomach feels like a bowl of very sloppy yoghurt.'

'Don't look down,' said Hubert. 'Keep your eye on the cave-mouth. Come on.' He held out a helping hand and gently guided the great creature higher. Once again Belinda was touched at Hubert's care and kindness. I don't deserve him, she thought. He's too kind. But of course she did deserve him really, and she looked after him in her own way, so they were well suited.

They reached the hole in the rock and hauled themselves over the edge. 'Phwooor!' cried Hubert, holding his nose. 'This place stinks!' A revolting smell of old cabbage and boiled eggs

drifted from the mouth of the cave.

'Ssssh, you'll wake the MoNsta,' whispered the princess and she tiptoed forward, following the string. The cave was very dark and they paused for a few moments until their eyes grew used to the lack of light, but even then they could hardly see a thing. As they pressed deeper into the cave the smell became ever more powerful and they clenched their hands over their faces.

Some distance behind them, and keeping well out of sight, Prinz Blippenbang darted from rock to rock as he carefully tailed the four MoNsta hunters.

Gordon was right about the size of the cave. The roof quickly soared higher and higher. The place was like a gigantic hall. Fat stalagmites sat dotted about the floor like grumpy old men, fast asleep. From the ceiling long thin stalactites were still dripping with water.

'It's so beautiful,' whispered Hubert. 'I wish I could stop and paint it all. It would make a wonderful picture.'

63

'I think we ought to sort out this beastie thing first,' Belinda answered. 'We're almost there. Keep very, very quiet.'

They rounded a big outcrop of rock and there in front of them was the MoNsta, fast asleep. It had a peaceful smile on both of its faces and it was breathing quietly and slowly, its great belly heaving up and down. The string was still tied round the end of its tail. A strange smoke seemed to drift away from the beast as it lay there, as if it was smouldering. But it wasn't smoke – it was pure MoNsta pong. The horrible odour rose from the body in great wafts and clung in the air.

Hubert turned to Knackerleevee. 'I used to think you smelled a bit sometimes, but this is the stink to end

all stinks.' The Bogle grunted. He was not sure if Hubert had said something nice or not.

For almost five minutes the companions just stood and gazed at the sleeping hulk, overwhelmed by the sheer size of the beast. Finally they withdrew a little and crouched down behind a large stalagmite.

'What's the plan?' asked Knackerleevee.

Belinda raised a cross eyebrow. 'Do I have to think of everything? My idea was the string-thing. Now it's somebody else's turn to think. My brain's having a rest.'

The Bogle and Hubert gazed at each other. Neither of them had a weapon, and the MoNsta was far too big to manhandle in any way at all. They were filled with deep depression – to have risked life and limb to get this far and then find they couldn't kill the beast! It was monstrous!

Gordon the goatherd was standing up and leaning across the side of the stalagmite, staring intently at the MoNsta. He seemed to have overcome his grief, and now anger was taking over. His bony fingers gripped the edge

of the stalagmite like fierce talons. His dark eyes were hard and shining and they fixed the beast with murderous intent.

'That horrible heap ate my goats,' he hissed. 'It ate Mirabel and Flossy and Duncan and Bert and Barnaby and little Trixie and, and . . . every single one of them.'

'Don't think about that now,' said Belinda softly, alarmed by Gordon's rising voice. 'Sit down and help us think of a plan to get rid of it.'

But Gordon pulled his arm away and hissed back at her through grimly gritted teeth. 'I don't need a plan. That goat-gobbler is a murderer!' With this final cry Gordon pulled a short sword from his belt and strode straight for the beast.

'Stop – you'll be killed!' warned Hubert, but Gordon carried on.

It was truly pitiful, and it made the three companions want to weep. Gordon had no chance at all. He was a thin, scrawny man with

nothing except a sword in his hand and anger in his heart, yet here he was marching on the beast. Belinda and Hubert and Knackerleevee held their breath. They almost stopped breathing altogether as they watched with mounting horror and fascination.

Every so often the MoNsta would flick open one eye. It was impossible to say where it would look. Sometimes Gordon nipped behind a pile of bones. Sometimes he just froze, as if he were one of the stalagmites in the cave. And somehow he managed to creep closer and closer.

The MoNsta flicked open an eye and stirred. It let out a thunderous belch and then slumped back into a doze again. Gordon took three more steps and now he stood right beside one of the huge heads. It was revolting. The scales were dull and flecked with blood. From the slit of a mouth several teeth poked out and some still had bits of goat fur stuck to them. Gordon's rage seized hold of him, giving him the power of ten men. He raised his sword above his head, grasping the solid handle with

both hands, and plunged it
down into the MoNsta's
skull.

The great neck and
head twitched,
throwing Gordon to
one side, but he was
up on his feet again,
running furiously to
the second head,
which was
stirring into
wakefulness. But
before the MoNsta
could react
Gordon had straddled the beast's neck, raised
his sword a second time and dispatched the
beast for ever. The MoNsta gave a huge groan,
lifted its second head for a last time and
crashed to the ground.

'Incredible!' whispered Belinda, her face
flushed with admiration. 'You've killed the
MoNsta, Gordon. Well done!'

The friends crowded round the goatherd,

patting him on the back, ruffling his hair and tweaking his beard. Gordon however felt flat and exhausted. All the fight had gone out of him, and now that he realized what danger he had been in he suddenly felt scared, even though there was nothing left to be scared about.

'This is excellent,' declared Belinda. 'Gordon has killed the MoNsta, so Gordon wins Taloola's hand and the million gold coins. What could be better?'

A deep voice from the far end of the cave surprised them all. 'Oh, I have a much better ending,' said Prinz Blippenbang.

'What? Who's that? Come out of the shadows,' cried Belinda, already bristling with a premonition that further danger was afoot.

The Prinz took several steps forward, his bazooka balanced over one shoulder and pointing at the friends. 'Allow me to introduce myself. I am Prinz Blippenbang and I have come to claim the MoNsta's heads. So kind of you all to lead me here, and even kinder of you to kill it for me. I do so hate getting my hands

dirty. Don't move a muscle!' he cried as
Belinda took a couple of angry steps towards
him. 'This is a bazooka, a very powerful
weapon, and you will do exactly as I say. You
there!' The Prinz gestured at Gordon. 'Goat-
boy! Cut off the MoNsta's heads, put them in
these sacks and bring them to me. Hurry!'

Gordon could only do as he was told while
the others watched in stunned silence. The
heads were stuffed into the sacks and laid at
Blippenbang's feet. The Prinz grabbed them
with his free hand and laughed loudly. 'I am
going to enjoy myself,' he
bragged. 'I shall go back to the
castle and tell that stupid
pumpkin of a Duke what a
terrible battle I had. I shall
show him the heads and
he will be so
pleased! Then
he'll give me a
million gold coins
and I shall be rich for ever!'

'What about Taloola?' cried Gordon.

'Oh hang Taloola! Taloola's a fat, ugly tub.'

'No she isn't! She's the most beautiful woman I have ever laid eyes on!' Gordon declared.

'Oh do shut up, you grubby goat-goon.' The Prinz began to back out of the cave. 'I'm sorry I have to dash off now, but unfortunately, because you all know the truth of what has happened here, I must leave you behind. I shall tell the Duke how the MoNsta had crunched you up in front of my very eyes before I could kill it.'

'You're not going to kill us are you?' Hubert had turned very pale.

'Um . . . not exactly. However, I would so much like to show you how powerful my bazooka is, so I am going to fire it at the cave roof here. The roof will come tumbling down and what a tragedy, you'll be trapped, for ever. What a shame. Boo hoo.'

'You're a monster!' cried Belinda. 'Worse than the MoNsta monster!'

'You say such nice things,' replied Blippenbang sweetly. 'Oh well, I really must be

going. So nice to have met you.'

With that the Prinz backed away to the entrance, turned his bazooka on the cave roof and pulled the trigger. Flames shot from the cannon. There was a deafening bang and moments later rocks began cascading down. Big boulders, little boulders, stalagmites that had taken thousands of years to grow, all came crashing down. They piled up at the entrance, rapidly rising, blocking out what little daylight there was until – nothing. Just darkness.

'Oh dear,' muttered the Karate Princess. 'I think we're trapped.'

7 Rabbits and Other Revelations

'Can you see anything?' asked Knackerleevee.

'No,' grumbled the others.

'Neither can I. Thank goodness.'

'What do you mean – "thank goodness"?' Hubert snapped. 'We're trapped halfway up a mountain in a deep cave, with no food and in total darkness. Why are you thanking goodness?'

'Because I thought I might have gone blind, but if nobody can see then I know that it's just got a bit darker.' The Bogle stumbled forwards, feeling his way with waggling, hairy fingers.

'Oi!' cried the goatherd. 'Watch where you're putting your great hairy hands. That was my bottom, if you don't mind.'

'Sorry,' muttered Knackerleevee. He took a step back, tripped over Belinda, tumbled backwards and sent Hubert sprawling, before finally falling flat on his face himself. The cave rang with angry and painful cries. It got even

worse as they struggled to their feet, reaching out, hitting others accidentally and knocking them down again.

'Stop!' cried Belinda. 'Just keep still – everyone! This darkness is hopeless. Let's just all sit down where we are, one by one. Hubert – sit down.'

'I'm sitting.'

'Gordon, sit.'

'I'm not a dog,' complained the goatherd.

'SIT! Knackerleevee, you sit down next, and now me. There, no accidents. Right, we are in a very nasty situation. Has anyone got any ideas as to how we get out?'

'If we feel around we could find the string and follow it to the entrance,' suggested the Bogle. 'Then we might be able to move the rocks out of the way.'

'Hmmm. I think the rock-pile brought down by Blippenbang is far too dense. It would take weeks to get through, and we haven't got weeks. Hubert – any ideas?'

'I agree with Knackerleevee.'

'You do?' The Bogle was definitely surprised to hear this.

'The way we came in is the only way in, so it must be the only way out,' Hubert said logically. 'We shall simply have to dig for our lives.'

'OK, it's agreed then.' Belinda nodded. 'Get down on your hands and knees and try and find the string.'

'You haven't asked me yet,' Gordon

muttered sulkily.

'Oh, sorry. Gordon! Have you got an idea?' asked Belinda brightly and waited for him to say 'No'. She knew he was angry with her for shouting at him.

'Yes, I have, and it's better than your idea too.'

'What is it?'

'Why should I tell you?' he asked sulkily.

'Because if you don't we shall all die in this cave with nothing but a stinking dead MoNsta for company and Prinz Blippenbang will get the money that you deserve AND he'll get Princess Taloola and he doesn't love her like you do and she'll be so unhappy she'll probably never eat again and pine away to nothing and die.'

'That'll take a long time,' remarked Knackerleevee darkly, and promptly received a kick from the princess. 'Sorry,' he added.

'All right, I'll tell you,' said Gordon. 'At the back of this cave there is a narrow passage that leads to the top of the cliff. That's how I managed to rescue my goat.'

'You mean there's another way out?!'

'Yes.'

'Why didn't you tell us?' cried Hubert.

'I just have.'

'But I thought you climbed up here from the bottom.'

'No, I never said that. I climbed down here from the top.'

'Surely we should be able to see a chink of daylight if there's a passageway to the top?' asked Belinda.

'The MoNsta's tail is blocking it off,' said Gordon. 'I'll lead the way. We shall have to hold each other's feet so that we don't lose contact.'

So Knackerleevee held on to Hubert's ankles, and Hubert held on to Belinda's ankles, and she held on to the goatherd's ankles, and off they went, like a choo-choo train, puffing and grunting and hissing with effort. It did not take them long to reach the MoNsta's tail, and with a lot of one, two, three and HEAVE! they pushed the tail out of the way and revealed a narrow, perpendicular chink of light.

'Gordon – you are very clever,' announced Belinda. 'Let's get going, and let's hope that we are not too late.'

Dudless, Duke of Dork didn't know whether to laugh or cry. 'The MoNsta's dead! No more weeping and wailing. No more danger. No

more hiding in paper bags. Oh, but poor Dorinda – what a way to go. Crunched to bits, you say?' Prinz Blippenbang nodded.

'I tried my best to save them, but . . .' He looked suitably upset. The Duke patted the Prinz on one shoulder.

'There, there. Everyone knew the risk they were taking, eh? I shall write to my brother and let him know. Poor Dorinda.' The Duke was silent for a few moments and then he brightened up a bit. 'But you're alive! That is good news. Do you know? I think I'm going to treat myself to a new pet rabbit. And what shall I call him?' The Duke's gaze rested fondly on his new-found hero, the wonderful MoNsta-masher, Prinz Blippenbang. 'I shall call him Bloppenpop, after you!'

'How kind,' said the Prinz, smiling. 'Now, about those million gold coins . . .'

'All in good time, dear thing, all in good time. I expect you want to be with the blushing bride. Taloola, do stop snivelling and snuffling. Look what a fine prize you have here. Prinz Bloppenpop is so strong, and handsome.'

'I loved Gordon the goatherd. He was sweet and kind and had a wispy beard that tickled and now he's dead and gone and I shall never be happy again. Ohwohwoh!' And she burst into tears and threw herself on the settee.

'She'll get over it, dear chap,' said the Duke cheerfully.

'About the money . . .' hinted the Prinz again.

'Yes indeed, all in good time, but we must have a wedding, and a wotchamacallit, you know, where everyone goes round . . .'

'Merry-go-round?' suggested the Prinz.

'No, no, everyone goes round and they do

things with their feet . . . a football, no, that doesn't sound quite right. It's on the tip of my tongue you know.'

'Do you mean a ball,' suggested Blippenbang. 'Where everyone dances?'

'That's it! That's it. What a clever chappie you are. Brains and muscles eh? Yes, we must have a Grand Ball tonight to celebrate the Defeat of the MoNsta, and then the wedding and your million gold coins.'

Prinz Blippenbang smiled politely. 'Lovely idea, but I don't suppose I could have the money before the wedding?'

'No, no, that will be my wedding present,' said the Duke. 'Surely you don't expect me to give you a million gold coins and a wedding present? That would be greedy! Now, do excuse me Bloppenpop, I must go and organize the ball.'

Prinz Blippenbang ground his teeth together and watched the stout little Duke hurry away. What a stupid man he was. So, he would have to marry Taloola before he got the money? Oh well, no matter. He would just have to ditch

her after the wedding instead of before it. He went to his room to prepare for the dance.

To be fair to the Duke it must be admitted that he pulled out all the stops for the Grand Ball. The entire castle was decked out with flowers and balloons and a huge feast had been prepared. Everyone was invited. Ladies pulled out their finest gowns and the castle was filled from cellars to attics with laughter and song and relief and joy that they were out of danger at last.

Only two people were not sharing in the merry-making. Taloola moped about the hall with tears streaming down her puffed-up face. Meanwhile Prinz Blippenbang tugged on his best dancing jacket. He was wondering how quickly he could get the money from the Duke.

The band arrived and set up at one end of the great hall. Music rose into the air with a

twirl and a flourish and soon numerous feet were skipping and turning and twirling and bouncing as the excited guests danced their socks off.

Outside in the fragrant evening, four weary travellers hurried towards the sound of music and the glittering lights of the celebrating castle. 'I do hope we're not too late,' said Hubert. 'Come on Knackerleevee, hurry up.'

'I've got a stitch,' complained the Bogle, sitting on the ground and clutching one side. 'You go on. I'll catch you up.'

Belinda and the others hurried back to him. 'You two take his arms. I'll take his legs. Come on.'

Before the Bogle could protest he found himself being carried at a trot towards the castle, bouncing up and down like a big piece of carpet. When they arrived at the drawbridge they were met by several guards brandishing crossed spears.

'We want to go inside,' declared Belinda.

'Oh yes? Where's your invitation?'

'You're not even wearing a ball gown,'

sneered a second guard.

'I haven't got a ball gown,' said Belinda.

'There you go then. You can't come in. And pick that bit of carpet up before you leave.'

'This is becoming very boring,' warned Belinda. 'Are you going to let us through or not?'

'Definitely not,' said the third guard, smiling.

'I think you ought to do as she asks,' said Hubert helpfully. 'Otherwise she might do something rather unpleasant.'

'Ooh, we are scared!' cried the guards.

'What's she going to do? Blow a raspberry!'

Hubert and Knackerleevee covered their eyes. Gordon, who had never seen the Karate Princess in action, watched in amazement. He had never seen such a battering, flattening, denting, headache-making, stunning display.

'Ha-akk!' cried Belinda as she made mincemeat of the three guards, and cast them one by one into the cold, wet moat below. 'Happy fishing!' she cried as she crossed the drawbridge and marched into the great hall. She went straight up to the dance band, grabbed the biggest drum she could find and banged it and banged it until the music stopped, the dancers stopped, and all eyes were on her.

Prinz Blippenbang was visibly shaken and now Belinda pointed an accusing finger at him. 'Uncle, that man is a cheat, and a would-be murderer. He's about as much a hero as a jar of jam.'

The Duke was in a tizzy. He could make no sense at all of what was happening. 'Um, Dorinda, you're dead, aren't you? What are you doing here? And what kind of jam were you thinking of?'

'Uncle! It doesn't matter about any jam and I'm not dead, even though the Prinz tried to kill me and my friends. He's claiming that he killed the MoNsta, but he didn't. He was too

scared to go anywhere near the beast.'

This pronouncement really set tongues wagging. The brave Prinz not brave at all? What was going on? And where was the Prinz anyway?

Blippenbang was no fool. He could see the way things were going. But he was determined not to lose out on the million gold coins. He raced up the stairs to his room to fetch his trusty bazooka.

8 And Did They All Live Happily Ever After?

Prinz Blippenbang burst into his room, but someone had beaten him to it.

'Looking for something?' asked Hubert, pointing the bazooka at the cursing Prinz. 'I think we had better go back downstairs, don't you? You go first.' Blippenbang had no alternative but to head back down the stairs, looking thunderous.

'Will somebody please tell me what's going on?' squeaked the Duke when he saw the Prinz being escorted into the hall. Belinda explained, recounting the whole story, from the moment they set off to fasten the string to the MoNsta's tail, right up until when they got back to the castle. Dudless, Duke of Dork, listened to the tale with growing anger.

'Is this true?' he demanded of the Prinz.

'What if it is?'

'Don't you even love my beautiful daughter?'

'Pah! Beautiful? I'd rather marry a camel!'

At this point Gordon the goatherd almost threw himself on the Prinz, but it was Taloola who held him back. She walked over to the Prinz and gazed up into his blue eyes. 'I may not be a beauty as considered by some people,' she said with great dignity. 'I'm so sorry I displease you, Prinz Blippenbang. Please, excuse me.'

Taloola turned gracefully away, then all at once whirled round and delivered such a stunning slap to the Prinz's face that he staggered back several paces, clutching his cheek. Taloola made the Prinz an elegant curtsy and went back to her admiring goatherd. The dancers cheered and Blippenbang crept away like a bruised snake, thoroughly outwitted and shamed into the bargain.

Dudless was still spluttering with confusion.

'Will somebody please tell me who killed the MoNsta? If it wasn't Bottompop then who was it?'

'Gordon the goatherd!' everyone cried.

'Gordon? But he's a vegetarian. I thought he didn't believe in killing animals.'

'I'm afraid I lost my temper,' said Gordon sheepishly. 'The MoNsta killed all my goats, and I was very angry.'

'Quite so,' said the Duke, patting Gordon on the back affectionately. 'But never mind. We shall get you some more goats and, and rabbits too! Do you like rabbits? I love 'em. I'm going to get a new rabbit, and I shall call it Gordon, after you, my brave little rabbit.' This produced more clapping and cheering, but the Duke hadn't finished.

'Well now, if you killed the MoNsta then you win the prize, and I hope you'll be, ooops, there they go already! There's no stopping young love!' He stepped back hurriedly as Taloola flung herself into Gordon's arms, bearing him backwards at full speed until at last they crashed into the band.

'Ah music!' cried the
Duke. 'That's what we
need, more dancing.
On your feet
everyone! Dorinda,
go and put on one
of the Duchess's
outfits, they should fit you all right. Hubert,
you're fine. Hmmm, I don't know about the
Bogle. A bit of lipstick maybe?'

'I don't think so, Uncle,' laughed Belinda.
'Leave him as he is. Besides, he won't want to
dance. He gets the stitch you know.' She
hurried upstairs to the Duchess's dressing room
and there she found outfits galore. The
Duchess herself was sitting in the corner, doing
a jigsaw puzzle. She seemed only slightly
surprised that Belinda was going through her
best clothes, but was too busy trying to find a
missing jigsaw piece to take the cheese out of
her ears and actually ask what she was doing.

Belinda pulled out the garments one by one
and looked at them. She held them in front of
her and gazed into a mirror. Belinda didn't like

balls. She preferred racing round chipping and chopping and having exciting adventures, but she knew she couldn't do that all the time. She supposed she would have to try on one of the outfits and go back down to the dance.

Belinda chose the best one, pulled it on, sighed and went downstairs. The moment she appeared she was surrounded by handsome princes, all asking for the first dance, but she only had eyes for Hubert.

'You look stunning,' he said, smiling.

'I am stunning,' answered the Karate Princess. 'I do an awful lot of stunning. I stunned those guards outside this evening, if you remember.'

'I do, and now you've stunned me too,' said Hubert, blushing. 'Would you like to dance?' And the happy couple went tripping and crashing and bumping and banging all the way across the dance floor.

The reason for all this crashing and banging was that Belinda was probably the most hopeless dancer in the world. She was excellent at karate. She could speak four different

languages. She could make a mean omelette and chips. But dancing was simply not one of her talents. When Belinda went dancing in a crowded ballroom, it was like watching a team of expert tree-fellers at work. You could tell exactly where she was because the other dancers were falling over all around her, like trees in a forest being cut down in one sweep. The other dancers were tripped over by her feet, nudged by her elbows, and toppled by her barging shoulders.

Within a couple of minutes the dance floor was a writhing mass of fallen bodies, and only Hubert and Belinda were still on their feet. 'What's happened to Taloola and Gordon?' asked the princess.

'I think they're busy,' said Hubert, grinning, and pointed across to the dance band. The two lovebirds were sitting surrounded by violin players. They were holding hands and gazing rapturously into each other's eyes. Everyone in the room discreetly turned away and began talking about the weather.

'What a lovely morning!' cried a blushing Duke.